Six are they, the Badgers' Crowns

If power ye seek, they must be found

Crystal, iron and flaming fire

Gather them, if ye desire

Ice, and wood and carven stone

The power they give

Is yours

Alone

SUNDERED LANDS

FIRE OVER SWALLOWHAVEN

BY ALLAN FREWIN JONES
AND GARY CHALK

ILLUSTRATIONS BY

GARY
CHALK

Hodder
Children's
Books

A division of Hachette Children's Books

The Sundered Lands Chronicles:

Trundle's Quest

Fair Wind to Widdershins

Fire Over Swallowhaven

The Ice Gate of Spyre

Sargasso Skies

Full Circle

Prologue

The legends say that once, long, long ago, there was a single round world, like a ball floating in space, and that it was ruled over by six wise badgers. The legends also tell of a tremendous explosion, an explosion so huge that it shattered the round world into a thousand fragments, a vast archipelago of islands adrift in the sky. As time passed, the survivors of the explosion thrived and prospered and gave their scattered island homes a name – and that name was the Sundered Lands.

That's what the legends say.

But who believes in legends nowadays?

Well . . . Esmeralda Lightfoot, the Princess in

Darkness does, for one. According to Esmeralda, the truth of the ancient legend was revealed to her in a reading of the Magical and Ancient Badger Blocks. And her reluctant companion Trundle Boldoak is beginning to believe, as well – especially as they have already found two of the crowns. They have also found a new friend to accompany them on their quest – a light-hearted minstrel by the name of Jack Nimble.

But there is a problem. Someone else is also hunting for the six crowns – his name is Captain Grizzletusk, and he's the meanest, bloodthirstiest, wickedest pirate ever to sail the skies of the Sundered Lands. And just to make matters even worse, Grizzletusk and his murderous pirate band are being controlled by none other than Millie Rose Thorne, Queen of all the Roamanys, and – horrifyingly enough – Esmeralda's very own aunty.

No wonder our heroes are on the run!

Swallowhaven

'Keep hold of that feather, Trundle!' yelled Esmeralda. 'If it gets away from you, we're done for!'

'I *am* keeping hold of it,' Trundle replied, between gritted teeth. 'It's not easy, you know! The thing's got a mind of its own.'

He was quite worn out with the effort of hanging on to the long red phoenix feather. It strained forward over the prow of their skyboat, *The Thief in the Night*, twitching and twisting and squirming in his aching paws as if it were desperate to break free and soar away into the night.

With the help of a friendly hedgehog called the Herald Persuivant – or Percy for short – Trundle, Esmeralda and their companion Jack Nimble had discovered the feather in an old clock tower in the ancient city of Widdershins, coiled up in a metal orb attached to the Iron Crown of the Badgers of Power.

Jack had recognized the feather at once and sung them the song of the lovely and glorious phoenix bird, which, if its feather were returned, would tell a Great Secret. Of course, Esmeralda was instantly certain that the secret of the phoenix must be the clue that would lead them to the third of the Six Crowns of the Badgers of Power: the Crown of Fire.

And so, leaving the Crystal Crown and the Iron Crown for safekeeping with Percy, they had set off to find the phoenix. According to legend, the wonderful bird lived inside a volcano on a desolate and far-flung island at the furthermost reaches of the Sundered Lands.

Well, of course he does, Trundle had thought the moment he heard this. It would be too *easy* if he lived somewhere normal!

And so they had set off for the fiery mountain home of the mythical phoenix bird. It seemed to Trundle that the further they went, the more impatient the feather became to find its way home. But their trim little skyboat was *already* whizzing along as fast as possible. Esmeralda was at the tiller and Jack was racing to and fro with the boom, the pair of them expertly catching every last breath of wind so that the sails were stretched almost to bursting point, and the slender hull went zipping through the night like an arrow from the bow.

'If you can't hold that feather any longer,'

puffed Jack as he hauled on the thrumming ropes, 'why don't you try nailing it to the mast?'

'Brilliant notion!' exclaimed Trundle. He chose not to add that it was a pity Jack hadn't thought of that a while ago, and saved him cramped paws and strained muscles from the effort of keeping the rebellious feather under control.

Needing both hands free for this task, Trundle unbuttoned his jerkin and shoved the wriggling feather inside. Buttoning himself up again, he rummaged in the pile of goods and provisions that was heaped up in front of the mast.

'*Hee hee hee*,' he chortled, doubling up.

'What are you playing at, Trundle?' called Esmeralda.

'I'm – *hee hee hee* – I'm looking for a – *hee hee* – a hammer and – *ho ho, ha ha ha* – and a nail – *hee hee hee*,' Trundle replied, wriggling and writhing

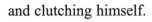

and clutching himself.

'What's so funny?'
Esmeralda demanded.

'The feather – *hee hee hee* – it's tickling me,'
gasped Trundle, tears rolling down his face.

'Oh, for heaven's sake!'
exclaimed Esmeralda. 'This is a serious quest, Trundle. Stop larking about!'

Stifling his giggles, Trundle managed to find a hammer and a nail. He took the feather out, held it against the mast, and with a few quick whacks drove a nail into the wood and bent it over so that the shaft of the feather was trapped underneath.

Cautiously, he let the feather go. It quivered and shook itself like a dog coming out of the water. For a moment, Trundle got the distinct feeling the feather was looking reproachfully at him – if such a thing were possible. Then it seemed to gather itself again and stretched out as taut as a bow-string, pointing forward into the starry sky.

With a gasp of relief, Trundle turned and sat himself down with his back to the mast. At last he could relax and give his paws and arms a rest.

'Oi, lazybones!' shouted Esmeralda. 'No slacking, there! If you've got nothing better to do, make us some sandwiches. Treacle, for me, please – and make it good and thick. I'm famished!'

With a sigh, Trundle set to.

It was a beautiful dawn. *The Thief in the Night* soared through a sky banded with orange and saffron and rosy clouds. Fresh, tangy air blew into Trundle's excited face as he gazed around in pure joy. The sky was dotted with distant islands in all directions, some just dark spots on the edge of sight, others lit up by the rising sun and glittering like tiny jewels hanging in the endless blue.

It was at times like this he was glad he had given in to that moment of madness back on his homeland of Shiverstones and agreed to accompany the crazy Roamany girl on her madcap quest. The adventures he'd had! The places he had seen!

And rising up swiftly beneath them was yet another spectacular and breathtaking sight: a great island-city that stretched almost as far as the eye could see. As the morning sun came out from behind the dark floating mass of Nightreef, its rays glanced on orange and terracotta roof tiles, glowed on yellow and white walls and crept across wide paved plazas and squares. It shone on marble statues and gushing fountains; it flashed off tall arched windows and lit up elegant towers and spires and domes of white and green and

pink marble, where gallant silken banners floated in the breeze.

Jack put an arm around Trundle's shoulders.

'Swallowhaven,' he sighed, gazing down at the approaching island. 'Balm of the weary soul, solace to the sore eye, comfort to the aching foot! It must be five years since last I was here.'

Trundle could understand Jack's enthusiasm – Swallowhaven was a wonderful and spellbinding vision in the early-morning light. The vast city lapped up to the very brink of the island. There were even buildings that perched precariously over the outermost edge, their windows and verandas and graceful balconies staring down into blue nothingness.

Quays, piers and jetties of white stone hemmed the outer rim of the city, while here and there, wharves and docks snaked inwards, their moorings teeming with a colourful multitude of windships and skyboats.

The travellers had come to the sprawling trading city in order to pick up provisions. Although they had sky-charts to guide them, drawn up by the Guild of Observators in Widdershins, they would soon be heading out into regions marked with the comment: *Devoid of scientific interest*, which Jack told them simply meant no one had bothered exploring that far out from the sun before. And, as the phoenix feather was leading them right into the Devoids, as they started calling the area, they would need to take on plenty of fresh food and water for the rest of their trip.

As Esmeralda brought *The Thief in the Night* down in slow loops towards the city, Trundle saw that the sky below was teeming with swallows, skimming along on outstretched wings, darting from rooftop to rooftop, diving in under the eaves and then spilling out again in their dozens, their high trilling calls filling the warm air.

'It's quite delightful,' he said wistfully. 'So peaceful! What a pity we can't stay here for a while.'

A cautionary voice in his head whispered: *Be careful what you wish for, my lad!* But he ignored it.

Just then, a small navy-blue skyboat came sailing up towards them, its mast flying a bright golden flag.

'Aha,' said Jack. 'We're due a visit from the Grand Wardens, I see.'

'Who are they?' asked Trundle.

'You have to understand that this is a very formal society,' Jack explained. 'There are rules and regulations for everything you do. You can't make landfall here without getting permission from the Grand Master President of the Harbours.' He grinned. 'Everything is called the Grand this or that. It's all very silly, of course, but . . .' His voice trailed off. 'That's odd,' he said, a moment later.

Trundle peered down at the approaching skyboat. 'What is?'

'They weren't armed and armoured last time I was here,' mused Jack. 'Hmmm. I wonder what's up.'

There was no more time to speculate before the ornate skyboat came alongside *The Thief in the Night*. Trundle saw that the crew was clad in metal breastplates and wore ridged iron helmets. They looked stern and a little frightened, and they all carried long spears.

A fresh-faced young otter in golden livery stepped forward. 'I am Grand Junior Warden of the Great Eastern Spice Dock,' he announced. 'What is your business here?'

Esmeralda joined them at the bows. 'Hello there,' she chirruped merrily. 'We're just passing through, you know. We need food and water, that's all, then we'll be on our way.'

12

The Grand Junior Warden eyed her distrustfully. 'Is that so?' he said. 'Do you not know that the United Mercantile Principality of Swallowhaven is on a war footing, and that anyone approaching our city without express permission of the Merchant Princes is liable to be thrown into jail without trial or hearing?'

'Lawks!' exclaimed Jack. 'No, we didn't know that.'

The Grand Junior Warden raised an eyebrow. 'Well, you do now.' He lifted an ebony baton. 'In the name of the Grand Master President of the United Alliance of Merchant Princes, I commandeer this vessel and demand that all who sail in her be secured and held incommunicado under the Articles of War!'

'Here, hold on!' said Esmeralda as the crewmen bristled menacingly at the Grand Junior Warden's back. 'We're innocent travellers. There's no need to take us prisoner!'

'Don't take it personally,' said the Grand Junior Warden. 'If you can convince the tribunal that you're not in league with the pirates, you'll probably be set free as soon as the battle is over.' He chewed his lower lip anxiously for a moment. 'Providing we win the battle, of course. If we lose it . . .' His shoulders slumped in a way Trundle found disturbing. 'Well, it really won't matter, will it? We'll probably be captured and sold into slavery – those of us who aren't slaughtered, executed, maimed, crushed, mangled or tossed off the edge of the island.'

'Um, excuse me a moment,' said Esmeralda. 'Did you say "pirates"? You don't by any chance mean a particular pirate captain who goes by the name of Grizzletusk, do you?'

The Grand Junior Warden's eyes narrowed. 'Aha! Then you *do* know him!'

14

'Well, we know *of* him,' Trundle added quickly.
'It's not like he's our chum or anything.'

'Quite the reverse, in fact,' said Jack. 'Truth to
tell, he's been chasing us for some time now.' He
nodded fervently. 'We're sworn and bitter enemies,
you know. Ask anyone.'

'I'm very glad to hear it,' said the Grand
Junior Warden.

'So what's old Grizzletusk up to?' asked
Esmeralda. 'No good, I'll be bound.'

'Word has reached us that he has assembled a
fleet of twenty-five windships,' said the Grand Junior
Warden. 'They're heading this way right now,
apparently, intent on plunder . . . and worse.'

'Lummee!' said Jack. 'Twenty-five, you say?'

The Grand Junior Warden nodded glumly.

'Er, what's going on down there?' asked
Esmeralda. Trundle and the others followed her gaze.

15

From all points along the margins of the city, windships and skyboats were rising in their hundreds into the sky, darting this way and that and skimming off into the distance like swarms of disturbed insects.

'That will be the last of the civilians heading off to safety before the battle gets going,' said the Grand Junior Warden. 'Just to be on the safe side, the old people and children and all of our most valuable treasures will be hidden away in Mousehole Reach, a little island half a day's sailing from here.' He nodded thoughtfully. 'You never know with pirates – they're a bad-tempered lot, so I'm told – and to be honest with you, none of us has a clue how to fight them.'

'We can help you there,' said Esmeralda, much to Trundle's alarm. 'Ever heard the name Razorback? He's Captain Grizzletusk's bo'sun – and an ugly, brutal piece of work he is, to be sure.' She pointed at Trundle. 'But this fine fellow beat him in a fair battle in the mines of Drune. Clipped his wings good and proper, he did!'

'Well, I wouldn't exactly say that,' Trundle began. 'Truth to tell—'

'No false modesty now, Trun,' interrupted Esmeralda. 'We might not look it, Mr Grand Junior Warden, sir, but we're brave and experienced warriors. If I were you, I'd take us straight to the commander of your armies – I'm sure we'll be able to help in the coming battle.'

'I like the sound of that,' said the Grand Junior Warden. 'And it'll save me a whole heap of paperwork, too. Very well, I will present you to the Grand Tribunal of Adjudicators. Follow me!'

And with that, he shouted some instructions to his men, whereupon the skyboat wheeled around and went looping down towards the city.

'What did you say that for?' Trundle demanded

of Esmeralda, as *The Thief in the Night* sailed down behind them to moor at Swallowhaven. 'We don't really know how to fight pirates either.'

'Think, Trundle,' she said. 'Would you rather they threw us straight into jail, or would you rather stay free?'

Jack chuckled and rubbed his hands together. 'Good thinking, Esmeralda,' he chortled.

'Hmmm,' grumbled Trundle. 'So with any luck we'll have time for a cream bun and a nice sit-down before we all get our throats cut by marauding pirates.'

'That's the spirit,' Esmeralda said, slapping him on the back. 'Always look on the bright side!'

Amazons, Wolves and Steammoles

The beautiful city of Swallowhaven was strangely quiet and empty as Trundle and the others were marched through the streets by the Grand Junior Warden and his squad. Trundle noticed a few people boarding up windows and nailing planks across doors, but apart from them and the occasional anxious soldier posted on a street corner, it seemed that everyone had fled the coming combat.

Trundle didn't blame them. He remembered

only too well the sight of diabolical pirates marauding through the streets of his hometown of Port Shiverstones, killing at random, setting fires in the wharves, firing their deadly cannon.

He shivered at the memory. He and Esmeralda had been running from the pirates ever since – and now it seemed that they had got themselves tangled up in someone else's war!

The Grand Junior Warden led them into the foyer of a stupendously huge and opulent building. Watched by the eyes of golden statues, they walked with echoing footsteps over marble floors. Diamond-encrusted figurines glittered on plinths and in alcoves. The walls soared up around them, decorated with frescos and murals and hung with silken flags. Peering upwards and feeling very, very tiny, Trundle saw the high arched ceiling was painted with cherub-piglets and vole-cupids and plump hamster angels, prancing and leaping among fluffy pink clouds.

'Rich people,' Jack murmured, looking appreciatively around. 'It's no wonder the pirates have got their eye on this island.'

They came though a high entranceway and into another long room. At the far end, five elderly animals in impressive robes sat on five high marble thrones.

The Grand Junior Warden bowed low. 'Most High and Puissant Castellans of the Grand Tribunal of Swallowhaven,' he began. 'I beg to interrupt your august deliberations for a moment in order to—'

'Oh, cut the cackle,' Esmeralda interrupted him, marching up to the five thrones and fixing the Tribunal with a gimlet eye. 'Listen, it sounds like you've got problems with pirates.' She gestured towards Trundle and Jack. 'There's nothing we don't know about pirates.'

The five Puissant Castellans stared at her with a

21

mixture of outrage and disbelief. Trundle guessed they weren't often spoken to like this.

'So, let's do a deal,' Esmeralda continued. 'We'll tell you all we know about how to fight pirates, on the condition you give us all the supplies we need and let us nip out the back way before the punch-up begins. How's that sound?'

The Puissant Castellan in the central throne – an elderly, grizzled bear with weak, watery eyes – leaned forward and stared down at her.

'You know all there is to know of the ways and means of battling pirates?' he asked in a quavering voice.

'Sure thing,' said Esmeralda. 'Ask away!'

The bear gazed past her. 'Junior Grand Warden, these animals must join our Invincible Fleet. Take them to the Grand Admiral Agrocrites Firwig. They will make excellent scouts in the coming strife.'

'Here, wait a minute,' Esmeralda exclaimed as several pairs of hands reached for her. 'That wasn't the plan at all!'

'So?' Trundle whispered pointedly. 'How exactly do you intend to get us out of this mess?'

Esmeralda frowned at him. 'Give me time. I'm thinking.'

'Thinking is good,' murmured Jack. 'Thinking before you talk us into trouble is even better.'

Esmeralda gave him a quick glare but said nothing.

'Do you think your aunty will be with the pirates?' asked Trundle, a shiver running down his spine as he remembered all the trouble that wicked old lady had caused them.

'Not her,' said Esmeralda. 'She'll be snug in her caravan, plotting horrible plots, if I know her. I think

23

this attack on Swallowhaven is probably all Grizzletusk's idea. A quick way to add to his coffers!'

They were back aboard *The Thief in the Night*, heading for one of the city's internal wharves. A Swallowhaven warden was at the tiller and another sat in the prow with a drawn sword across his lap. Escape was not an option.

Coming up fast on their starboard bow was a flamboyantly decorated five-masted galleon, with billowing golden sails and glittering gilt deck-rails. As they came closer, Trundle saw its name in gold leaf at the prow: *The Gilded Lily*.

He gazed at the gaudily adorned windship, thinking of *The Iron Pig* with its blood-red sails and its

 ironclad hull and its formidable cannon. Only the pirates knew

the secret of the exploding blackpowder that fuelled their cannon and their muskets and pistols. He could see this fancy galleon being blown into tiny fragments within five minutes of the battle getting started.

We're doomed, he thought. Totally doomed.

'Is this the only windship you've got?' Jack asked the warden at the tiller. 'Only – no offence, it doesn't really look up to engaging with *The Iron Pig*.'

'It was thought prudent to put as much of our wealth as possible beyond the reach of the coming enemy,' the warden replied stiffly. 'Most of the rest of the Invincible Fleet was mostly used to transport most of our treasures into hiding in Mousehole Reach.'

'Well, that was *mostly* a bit silly, wasn't it?' said Esmeralda. 'How exactly were you planning on fighting them?'

'We're rich,' the warden commented, with a snooty curl of the lip. 'We can afford to pay *other* people to do the actual fighting.'

They came alongside *The Gilded Lily* and the little skyboat was quickly secured. The wardens escorted Trundle, Esmeralda and Jack aboard the galleon and they soon found themselves on the forecastle, under the stern gaze of an elderly goat in a dazzlingly braided and bemedalled uniform. Above his long, mournful face, he wore a cocked hat spouting gold plumes.

'Admiral Agrocrites Firwig, I presume?' said Esmeralda. 'Are you in charge of this woeful excuse for a navy? You do know you're all going to be killed, don't you? If you'll take my advice, you'll pack your bags and head for Mousehole Reach as quickly as the wind will take you.'

Admiral Firwig adjusted his monocle. 'I don't think that will be necessary,' he announced. 'We have assembled a formidable fleet of paid soldiers.' He looked at Esmeralda and Trundle and Jack with a doubtful eye. 'I'm informed that you *persons* will be useful in the thick of the battle as scouts and expert observers.'

'In the thick of the battle?' echoed Jack in alarm. 'I'm not so sure about that.'

'Would you care to take a tour of our defences?' Admiral Firwig continued, ignoring Jack's comment.

'Yes – why not,' said Esmeralda. 'Show us what you've got, Admiral.'

Firwig muttered some orders to a nearby officer and a few minutes later, *The Gilded Lily* had set sail and was gliding on a curved course out from the city. Ahead of them, Trundle saw a row of ten windships hanging motionless in the sky, each with a chunk of powerstone secured to the mainmast. Not for the first time, he found himself marvelling at the properties of powerstone.

Without this extraordinary rock, there could be no sailing through the skies of the Sundered Lands; buoyant as cork in water, it allowed the windships and skyboats to float in the air. Every vessel had a chunk of powerstone onboard – usually kept in a wooden basket at the head of the mast. Any vessel that lost its powerstone was doomed to plunge down into the black, frozen nothingness that lurked in the unfathomable depths beneath the lowest of the islands.

'These are converted merchant vessels,' the admiral explained as they hove to, next to the becalmed fleet. 'As you will see, they are not entirely unprepared for warfare.'

The Gilded Lily sailed sedately along the front of the line of windships. They had names like *The Spice Gales*, and *The Sarky Cut*, and *Trades Increase*. Trundle could see that big rectangular shields had been arranged along the bows of the windships, and there were many archers and soldiers aboard.

'The archers' arrows have been dipped in dark lotus juice,' the Admiral explained proudly.

'Never heard of it,' said Esmeralda. 'What is it?'

'A poisonous brew made from the stamens and pistils of the dark lotus flowers, found only in the jungles of Spyre,' explained the admiral. 'Even the slightest scratch of a lotus-dipped arrow will cause hallucinations and hysterics and raving lunacy.'

'Hmm,' said Jack. 'Handy, that. But we were told that Captain Grizzletusk has a fleet of twenty-five windships. Even with that nifty juice, you're outnumbered two-and-a-half to one. And they have blackpowder!'

'This is merely the visible part of our fleet,' said the admiral. 'I will now show you the rest.' Another order sent *The Gilded Lily* speeding forward.

A loud female voice boomed out. 'Admiral

Firwig! Captain Dolly Wideawake seeking permission to come aboard the flagship, sir.'

'Permission granted!' the admiral called back. *The Gilded Lily* hove to, and the formidable figure of a badger in half-armour with a plumed beret at a jaunty angle on her head came swinging over on a bo'sun's chair: a contraption made up of a wooden seat suspended from ropes.

'And who are these little fellows?' boomed Captain Wideawake, fists on hips as she stared at Trundle and his friends.

'They are experts in the tactics and gambits required to fight pirates,' explained the admiral.

'Hurrumph!' snorted Captain Wideawake. 'Just let my Swallowhaven Amazons at 'em, that's all I ask. Why, the crew of *The Bolt from the Blue* could clear the skies of pirates single-handed, and that's a fact!'

'May I remind you, Captain, that your crew

consists entirely of ladies of the Guild of Seamstresses,' the admiral said mildly. 'Remarkable as they are, I feel a little extra help *might* come in useful. Would you care to accompany us to Underhaven so our newfound friends can meet our trusted allies?'

'I will, that,' said Captain Wideawake. 'Although whether soldiers whose loyalty can be bought for a hatful of sunders are going to prove trustworthy, we've yet to find out.'

'Captain Wilde and Captain Darkside are honourable animals,' said the admiral.

'Hurrumph!' said Wideawake.

The admiral ignored her. 'Make sail for Underhaven!' he called.

The Gilded Lily described a long graceful arc through the sky, turning to approach the city but steadily swooping lower and lower until Trundle realized they were going to sail right underneath the island.

They swept on, the underside of the island of Swallowhaven passing massively above them like a rugged and jagged ceiling – all craggy, barren rock honeycombed with caverns and pits and gullies. Hidden from the beams of the sun, it was a dark place where chill winds wafted and sneaked.

And then Trundle saw the two fleets of windships, lurking down there in the deep shadows. The closer fleet consisted of six wargalleons, painted bright red, armed with rams and fitted out with harpoon-launchers shaped like great crossbows. That looked more hopeful, he thought, although he also noted with a quiver of unease that the crews of these ships were made up of wolves and foxes.

'My old dad told me never to trust those creatures,' he whispered to Jack. 'He always said:

"While the wolf keeps you talking at the front door, the fox is busy in the larder."'

'These look a decent bunch,' Jack replied lightly. 'I think we should give them the benefit of the doubt.'

'Hmmm,' said Trundle dubiously.

As *The Gilded Lily* sailed by, a dandified wolf in a silver helmet launched himself from the poop deck rail of *The Scarlet Scavenger* and swung over on a rope. He landed lightly, sweeping the helmet from his head and bowing low.

'Captain Amery Wilde at your service,' he announced, with a flash of white teeth. He stepped forward, lifting Dolly Wideawake's plump paw and planting a kiss on it. 'A pleasure, as always.' He straightened up, his eyes sparkling with dash and brio. 'Admiral Firwig, my men are at your command. Give your orders and we will obey.'

'As soon as the pirate fleet appears, I want your windships to speed from cover,' said the admiral. 'Use your normal tactics, Captain – ram them, harpoon them and then board them.'

'It shall be done!' said Captain Amery with a flourish. 'We will smite them hip and thigh, Admiral, with sword, axe and halberd.' His eyes gleamed. 'And as we agreed, any ships we capture are ours to take and sell?'

'They are indeed,' said the admiral.

'Admirable!' said Amery Wilde. He smiled at Trundle and Esmeralda and Jack. 'Forgive my discourtesy, my fine fellows,' he said. 'I have pressing work to attend to, but I hope we will have time for introductions later. We shall drink together from the cup of victory when the battle is won!' And so saying, he caught hold of the rope again and swung back to his own windship.

'Well, he was a nice enough fellow,' said Jack. 'And a good chap to have with you in a tight corner, I dare say.'

Trundle nodded, reassured by Captain Wilde's breezy and friendly manner.

As *The Gilded Lily* sailed on, it became clear that the second of the secret fleets was a different proposition altogether. It consisted of four rather odd-looking windships, which seemed to be made entirely from dull grey iron. The hulls were of riveted iron strips, as were the decks and the featureless pilothouses – even the masts and the large powerstone baskets were iron. From the centre of each of the pilothouses jutted a strange iron funnel, spouting thick grey smoke. The curious windships were also strangely noisy: clankings and rumblings and clangings reverberated from their iron hulls. Trundle also noticed large, weirdly-shaped objects on the decks, hidden under grey tarpaulins.

The lead windship was called *The Black Velvet*.
Standing on the quarterdeck, small and grim in a frock
coat and two-cornered hat with a black cockade, was a
mole whose eyes were all but
hidden behind blue-tinted
spectacles. Their lenses were as
thick as the bottoms of bottles. The
silent crews of the four
windships were
also moles, clad
in grimy grey
dungarees and
tinted eye-
concealing
glasses.

'That is Captain
Thaddeus Darkside,' said the

admiral. 'Leader of the steammoles of Hammerland. His people live in the outer reaches of the Sundered Lands. We are very fortunate to have their support – they seldom concern themselves with events outside their own land. Captain Darkside tells me that beneath those tarpaulins he has some experimental weaponry that he is eager to test in combat. I have not seen the weapons, but he assures me they will come in most useful when battle is joined.'

'I don't like 'em steammoles,' grumbled Dolly Wideawake. 'You never know what they're thinking behind them glasses. Shifty, I calls it. Dead shifty.'

Staring out at the grimy, noisy, smoke-spewing iron windships, Trundle couldn't help but agree with her.

'So, twenty windships in all,' said Esmeralda. 'Against twenty-five pirate windships led by *The Iron Pig*.' She rubbed her chin. 'Hmmm. Interesting odds.'

'I bet you're wishing you hadn't talked us into this mess,' muttered Trundle. 'But maybe we can still slip away before things get uncomfortable. We *are* on an important quest, after all. There are four crowns yet to be found, remember? And this battle really doesn't have anything to do with us, does it?'

'He's got a point,' whispered Jack. 'What say we leg it while there's still time?'

Esmeralda looked from one to the other. 'Yes,' she said in an undertone. 'This time, I think you're both quite right. We need to skedaddle before Grizzletusk turns up.'

'How?' asked Trundle.

'I'm working on that,' Esmeralda replied.

'Sail ho!' called a lookout from the masthead of *The Gilded Lily*.

They turned to see *The Bolt from the Blue*

skimming swiftly towards them under the rocky ceiling of Swallowhaven island.

'Pirates!' yelled a frantic female voice from the prow of the onrushing windship. 'Cor, blimey, luvaduck! The pirates are here – flippin 'undreds of 'em, gawd 'elp us!'

And with that, *The Bolt from the Blue* came sailing up alongside *The Gilded Lily*. Captain Wideawake heaved herself up on to the rail and with a fearsome war cry, leaped back aboard her own foredeck.

'Needles in their nappers, my girls!' she hollered as *The Bolt from the Blue* turned, gathered speed again and rushed off to do battle. 'Pins in their posteriors! Scissors and pinking shears at the ready! Death or glory, Amazons of Swallowhaven – death or glory!'

Admiral Firwig turned to the three friends. 'Well, my young heroes,' he declared, 'it's time for you to prove your worth!' And with that, he shouted orders so *The Gilded Lily* cut a swift circle in the air and went flying out into the open skies.

'Oh, my giddy aunt!' gasped Trundle, his eyes bulging.

Filling the sky over Swallowhaven lay the entire pirate fleet – and at its head was the terrifying spectacle of Grizzletusk's flagship: the dire and dreadful *Iron Pig*!

Captain Grizzletusk

'So, my fine young beasts,' said Admiral Firwig,
lowering the telescope from his eye and turning to
Trundle, Esmeralda and Jack, 'battle is about to be
joined! Which tactics do you recommend?'

Run like fun! thought Trundle as he goggled at
the looming pirate fleet.

The Iron Pig with its grisly red sails was in the
lead, while the rest of the vessels – a motley and
mongrel bunch of windships, bristling with cannon and

sabre-wielding pirates – were organized in two long columns that stretched out like a pair of ugly ribbons in the flagship's wake. Already they were bearing down on the small Swallowhaven fleet like buzzards coming in for the kill.

'I've seen this formation before,' Esmeralda said grimly, gripping the rail as she stared at the approaching armada. 'They'll try to smash right through your fleet, blasting away with their cannon as they go. If your windships stay where they are, they'll be blown to smithereens.' She looked up at the admiral. 'Have you seen the damage the pirates' cannon can do? I have – and I don't recommend being in their sights once they start blazing away.'

'All your people will be killed if they don't get out of the way,' Jack added urgently.

'Then go tell them so!' said the admiral. 'Cast off *The Thief in the Night*,' he called. 'Admiral's orders: all windships to break ranks and hold off till reinforcements arrive.'

'Come on,' Esmeralda shouted to Trundle and Jack as she raced for their little skyboat. 'You heard the admiral – we've got work to do.'

Pausing only long enough to exchange a startled glance, the two of them went running after her.

As they leaped aboard, Trundle heard the admiral shouting further orders. 'Signal to Captain Wilde aboard *The Scarlet Scavenger*,' he bellowed. 'Tell him to lead his fleet into combat with all possible speed!'

'That'll give them piratical types a nasty surprise,' said Jack as he unfurled the sails. 'Jimminy, but this is exciting! I can feel a battle-song coming on!' He cleared his throat and began to sing:

Swallowhaven, stand ye steady,
Pirates come but you are ready,
Fight until they all are dead-ee,
Heroes one and all!

'Very stirring,' yelled Esmeralda, leaping for the tiller. 'Save it for later!' She grabbed the tiller in both hands and gave an almighty wrench. Its sails plump with the wind, *The Thief in the Night* went skimming away from the admiral's flagship.

Trundle clung to the mast, feeling the blood surging through his usually-peaceable veins. Curse those horrid pirates! It would serve them jolly well right if the whole darned lot of them were killed.

'Trundle, we're busy. You have to call to 'em to scatter!' yelled Esmeralda as they sped towards the Swallowhaven fleet. *The Bolt From The Blue* was back in line, and the pirate windships were bearing down on them in an arrowhead formation.

'They'll never hear me,' yelled Trundle.

'Improvise!' howled Esmeralda, leaning hard on the tiller.

What Trundle really needed was a megaphone – except that there wasn't one on board. Then he had a brainwave. He grabbed the copper tube in which their skycharts were kept rolled. Tipping out the charts, he leaned over the bow of *The Thief in the Night* and put one end of the hollow tube to his snout.

'Windships of Swallowhaven!' he bellowed at the absolute top of his voice. 'Split up! All of you! Get out of there! You'll be blown to bits otherwise!'

He spotted animals scuttling about frantically on the decks for a few moments, and then slowly but surely, the line of ten windships began to sheer off, left and right and up and down.

'Way to go, Trundle!' whooped Jack.

'Watch out!' shrieked Trundle. With the

Swallowhaven fleet scattered to the four corners of the sky, the only vessel remaining in *The Iron Pig*'s sights was theirs!

Jack flung himself across the skyboat, dragging the boom after him, while Esmeralda dug in hard with both feet and yanked the tiller almost out of its socket.

Trundle covered his eyes with his paw as *The Iron Pig's* blood-red sails filled the sky in front of them.

'Pop 'em, me hearties! Singe their eyebrows for 'em!' barked an all-too familiar voice. Trundle parted his fingers and saw that the fearsome bo'sun,

Razorback himself, was standing on the foredeck, yelling orders and brandishing his cutlass.

'It's them!' croaked yet another familiar voice. 'It's *them*, I tell 'ee! Kill 'em! Kill 'em to death, y'swabs!' Squatting on Razorback's shoulder was the scraggy black shape of his evil pet raven, Captain Slaughter. Except that, as Trundle noticed, the bird was looking a little the worse for wear since last they'd met. It had an eye-patch and a wooden leg, and a crutch under one wing – the result, Trundle guessed, of having been trodden on by his master in the heat of their fight in the verminous back-alleys of Rathanger, on the island of Drune.

'Let's give 'em a fright,' shouted Esmeralda at the tiller, her eyes shining. *The Thief in the Night* swooped down low over the deck of *The Iron Pig*, sending many a pirate diving for cover and making even Razorback and the raven duck to avoid having their heads knocked off.

'Shut your beak, you mangy magpie!' Trundle yelled down at the raven as they swept past.

'Blister me tripes!' bellowed Razorback. 'It *is* them! We searched the seven hundred skies of the Sundered Lands and they were here all the time!' He let out a laugh like a goose being strangled. 'Fortune favours the fiendish, ye stout-hearted stinkbugs! Twenty golden sunders for the man who captures them alive!'

This was followed moments later by a deafening volley of musket and pistol shot. The decks of *The Iron Pig* vanished in a fog of thick grey smoke. Trundle ducked and winced as musket balls went whistling past his ears. He heard the pop and crack of balls striking the skyboat's hull and searing through the sails.

But Esmeralda and Jack were a crack sailing

team, and while Trundle held on, whooping and hollering with excitement, they navigated *The Thief in the Night* down the full length of *The Iron Pig*, zigzagging in and out of the windship's masts and sending the crew leaping for their lives in all directions. They were flying so low that at one point Trundle was even able to give one pirate rat a hefty thwack around the ear with the copper tube.

'Ye lubbers!' roared a voice through the smoke. 'Ye bow-legged sons of cuttlefish! Blow 'em out of the sky! Must I do everything myself, blast yer eyes?'

The Thief in the Night surged upward as it neared the high poop deck, its keel scraping wood as it only just cleared the rail. And in the moment before they went scudding off, Trundle saw for the first time the frightful form of the leader of all the pirates of the Sundered Lands – the terrible and tremendous Captain Grizzletusk.

A huge and scarred hog he was, with a fearsome frowning brow and eyes as red and ferocious as blazing furnaces. His face was crisscrossed with scars and his jaw was twisted so that his hideous tusks jutted up crookedly, like the shards of a broken bottle. His right hand was missing, and in its place Trundle saw a great five-barrelled pistol sticking out from his sleeve, as though it were attached to the stump of his arm. He wore a leather belt and had two leather bandanas stretched over his mountainous chest, and into these were thrust swords and daggers and pistols and axes and choppers and maces and clubs and cudgels, so that he looked like an entire armoury on two thick-set legs.

He didn't even flinch as *The Thief in the Night* grazed past his head. Trundle saw him draw a massive pistol with his good hand. He aimed with both arms at them and, a moment later, six tremendous explosions

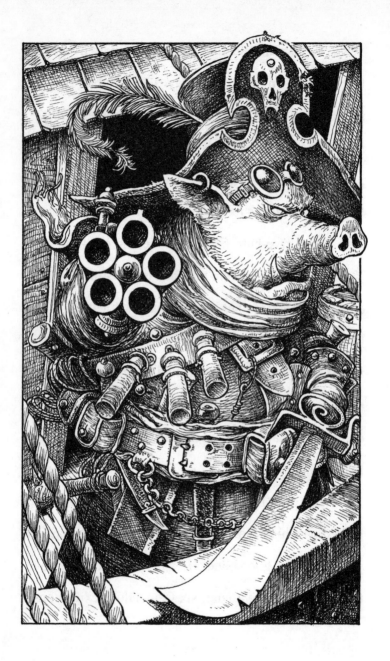

sounded as the ordinary pistol and the five-barrelled one went off at the same time. Trundle felt the heat of a musketball singe his prickles as Captain Grizzletusk vanished into a cloud of white smoke.

'Missed, you pitiful piglet,' Esmeralda shouted back. 'Missed by a mile!'

A split second later, it seemed to Trundle that the whole world was exploding around their ears.

'Oops!' shrieked Esmeralda as cannonballs came flying at them from all directions. In her excitement over getting clear of *The Iron Pig* she had forgotten that she was steering them right between two columns of heavily-armed and murderous pirate windships.

It seemed a great pity to Trundle, as red-hot cannonballs rocketed to and fro around him, that he wouldn't survive to tell her exactly what he thought of her navigating skills.

A Serious Punch-up!

'Hang on everybody!' yelled Esmeralda's voice, through the roaring of the guns and the hiss of the criss-crossing cannonballs and the billowing of the smoke. 'I'm going to try Escape Manoeuvre R.'

Trundle was about to ask what Escape Manoeuvre R involved, when suddenly *The Thief in the Night* seemed to stand on its nose and go plunging downward at breathtaking speed.

'Arrrrgggghhh!' he yelled as they burst out of the

cannon smoke and he found himself staring down in horror at a sky full of distant wheeling islands. The skyboat was falling vertically and spinning like a top. Jack was clinging on to the boom with one arm and clutching his precious rebec with the other, a fixed and manic expression on his face, while odds and ends from the skyboat were whisked away on the wind.

Esmeralda sat in the stern, grinning like a lunatic and ducking and dodging the debris as they plummeted. Then, just as Trundle gave himself up for dead, she stamped down hard on the boards and heaved at the tiller, her teeth gritted and her eyes screwed shut. With a sickening and stomach-twisting suddenness, the skyboat's prow lifted and it hurtled upward again. For a horrible moment, Trundle thought they were going to loop-the-loop, but then Esmeralda let out a yell of jubilation and suddenly the quivering *Thief in the Night* was on an even keel again.

'Whoooo!' Esmeralda hooted. 'That was fun! Shall I do it again?'

'Nooooo!' Trundle and Jack yelled in unison.

'Cissies!' Esmeralda shrieked with laughter. 'Now then,' she shouted, looking up, 'let's see how the battle is going.'

Trundle peered up. Above them, the arrowhead formation of the pirate fleet was still heading for Swallowhaven, but Admiral Firwig's brave little windships were darting in and out and back and forth, peppering the decks of the pirate windships with arrows and crossbow bolts.

'By crikey,' exclaimed Jack, jumping excitedly up and down, 'they're certainly giving those pirates something to think about. Good old Firwig!'

'And here comes Captain Wilde!' cried Trundle, punching the air as he spotted the six scarlet wargalleons with their rams and giant crossbows come shooting out from Underhaven, sails billowing.

'Hoorah! Hoorah! *Hoorah!*'

'And I only count twenty-one pirate ships,' said Jack.

'Oh, crumbs,' gasped Esmeralda. 'Look! *There* are the other four pirate windships – and they're sailing right out of the sun, the rotters. We have to go and warn the admiral or the Swallowhaven ships will be taken totally by surprise.'

A yank on the tiller and a swing of the boom and they were speeding upwards again towards the embattled Swallowhaven windships. It really was a dreadful sight! The pirate windships were constantly rocking back and forth from the recoils of their mighty cannon, and the whole sky seemed smeared and stained with puffs and swirls and streaks of smoke.

All of Admiral Firwig's vessels were engaged, but it was a very one-sided conflict. Even as Trundle watched, a fusillade of cannon fire ripped through the rigging and sails of *The Sarky Cut*. The mainmast cracked and snapped and to his horror, Trundle saw the basket of powerstone break loose.

At once, the stricken windship keeled over. Animals slid across the leaning decks to spill helplessly over the side, tumbling through the sky like autumn leaves. Slowly and horribly, the doomed windship began to fall, gradually gathering speed until it plunged past *The Thief in the Night* and went spiralling down and down until it was no more than a dot in the blue – and then, dreadfully, it was gone.

Enraged by the loss of all those lives, Trundle drew his sword and brandished it at the pirate windships. 'You cowards!' he raved. 'You murderers!'

Jack's hand rested on his shoulder. 'Try to keep your head, there's a good fellow,' the squirrel said gravely. 'People die in battles – the best we can hope to do is to avenge them.'

'Hey! What's going on now?' shouted Esmeralda. 'What's Amery up to?'

It was a question well worth asking. Four of the six scarlet wargalleons had gathered around *The Bolt from the Blue* and were bombarding it with massive wooden harpoons. The other two windships were speeding towards *The Iron Pig*. But far from ramming the pirate vessel, they slipped past it and joined in formation with the rest of the pirate fleet.

'The dirty filthy turncoats!' shrieked Esmeralda. 'They've changed sides!'

'I knew it!' howled Trundle. 'My old dad always told me never to trust wolves and foxes.'

'Oh, my, we're right in the soup!' groaned Jack. 'I'll never get the chance to write my battle song now.'

'Where are the steammoles?' cried Esmeralda. 'Why haven't they started fighting?'

Captain Wilde's treachery had clearly thrown the Swallowhaven windships into disarray. As *The Thief in the Night* at last came up level with the battle, Trundle saw *The Gilded Lily* darting this way and that, trying to avoid the fast-moving pirate windships that had come upon it out of the sun. These vessels seemed not to have cannon, but were smaller and lighter windships that darted above the larger, clumsier galleon, while the pirate crew lobbed grenades and bombs down on to its decks.

Clearly, Admiral Firwig was too preoccupied with keeping his vessel in one piece to be able to send the signal to *The Black Velvet* to join the battle. Captain Darkside and his four ironclad windships must still have been lurking in Underhaven, waiting to be called on.

'We have to get to the steammoles!' shouted Trundle. 'They're our only hope now!'

And a pretty feeble hope, too, he thought as *The Thief in the Night* tacked hard to starboard and went racing down into the cold gloom of Underhaven. They found the four sinister grey windships hanging in the air, their funnels belching dark smoke, their sides echoing with mechanical clanging.

Trundle put the copper chart-tube to his mouth again. 'Ahoy, Captain Darkside!' he shouted as they came up alongside *The Black Velvet*. 'Message from Admiral Firwig. The wolves have changed sides –

you're needed immediately or everything will be lost!'

As *The Thief in the Night* zipped in between the great unmoving windships of Hammerland, Trundle wondered for an alarming minute or two whether Thaddeus Darkside was going to do anything at all.

But then raucous sirens began to hoot and honk, metals bells clanged and clonged and a tremendous uproar sounded from beneath the grey iron decks of the four windships. Steammoles began to scuttle around the decks as the lumbering vessels clanked into slow, ponderous motion.

Trundle groaned. 'These great lumps of metal aren't going to be any use at all against the pirates.'

'Don't be so sure, Trundle, my lad,' said Esmeralda. 'Looks ain't everything! I've got a sneaky feeling there's more to these steammoles than meets the eye.'

'There'd need to be!' said Jack.

The four windships began to cleave through the air with a steady chugga-chugga-chugga noise that gradually got faster and louder until it was a continuous metallic screech that set Trundle's teeth on edge and gave him the feeling that someone was running nails down the inside of his skull.

And the Hammerland ships were quick, too! Much quicker than anyone aboard *The Thief in the Night* had expected. They quite took Esmeralda by surprise as they whizzed past, trailing thick plumes of white smoke. She twisted the tiller and they went speeding after the ironclad windships as they came out of the dark and into full sunlight.

As *The Thief in the Night* chased after the steammoles, Trundle saw that the tarpaulins were being drawn back off the lumpy shapes in the bows of the four windships. He stared at the weird devices that were revealed. Riveted to the decks, they were made of copper and iron with thick iron-ribbed pipes leading to and from them, and long metal nozzles that pointed out over the bows through slots in thick, curved iron shields. Trundle couldn't imagine what these great things were for. More than anything else, they reminded him of the old pump-handled fire engines that would be dragged through the streets of his hometown of Shiverstones: antique machines with handles that could be pumped up and down to send a spurt of water jetting into a burning building.

So, what were the steammoles planning – to squirt water at the pirates? Was *that* their secret weapon?

The Black Velvet was the first to engage with the pirates. And then Trundle learned the purpose of the strange machines!

Steammoles ran to either side and began to pump hard on the handles. A few moments later, great gouts of liquid flame came shooting out of the nozzles. The fire splashed across the first of the pirate vessels, setting rail and deck and rigging and mast and sail alight, all in a blazing moment!

The pirate windship went up like dry kindling and in no time at all it was ablaze from stem to stern. Burning like a torch, it began to spiral downwards, its ragged sails flapping like fiery wings as it plummeted.

By then, the other ironclad windships were busy among the enemy, spewing their deadly fires out over the pirate vessels and creating havoc and consternation among Captain Grizzletusk's astounded fleet.

'Oh, my word!' gasped Jack, his wide eyes reflecting the flames as Captain Darkside's fleet went jinking in and out of the columns of pirate windships, spraying fire and leaving mayhem in their wake. 'Have you ever seen the like?'

'No, never,' said Trundle with a shiver. 'I'm glad *they* didn't turn traitor!'

'Speaking of traitors,' exclaimed Esmeralda. 'I think Captain Wilde has bitten off more than he can chew. Let's go join in the fun!'

Trundle saw what she meant. *The Bolt from the Blue* had been harpooned by *The Scarlet Scavenger*, but Captain Wilde wasn't having things all his own way. In fact, from what Trundle could see, Dolly Wideawake's Amazons were giving Amery Wilde's crew a good walloping!

Whooping with battle-fever, Esmeralda steered them into the heart of the battle. As they drew closer, Trundle noticed that there was something not quite right about a couple of the pirate windships. They were no longer firing their cannon, but were just hanging in the air, doing nothing. And as they came alongside, he saw that the crews were behaving very oddly indeed.

Some of them had dropped their trousers and were waving their bottoms in the air, prancing about with wild abandon. Others were hitting themselves over the head with their own pistols. Yet more were hanging upside down in the rigging, laughing madly or singing, and a few were jumping overboard, flapping their arms like wings and chirping like birds as they hurtled downwards to their doom.

'I think we're seeing the effects of that dark lotus juice that Firwig mentioned,' said Jack. He grinned a savage grin. 'These Swallowhaven fellows aren't as helpless as they look, are they?'

'I'd say not,' breathed Trundle.

'Firwig, ho!' shouted Esmeralda as they came speeding up alongside the flagship of the Swallowhaven fleet. Another of Captain Wilde's scarlet wargalleons had smashed into the side of *The Gilded Lily* and the two were locked together. A lot of hand-to-hand fighting was going on.

'Let's get at 'em!' yelled Trundle, waving his sword and so filled to the brim with battle-fever that he quite forgot to be scared.

Esmeralda brought *The Thief in the Night* around hard and they made a bumpy landing on Admiral Firwig's foredeck.

With chilling war cries, the three brave animals leaped into the thick of the battle.

Ishmael March

'Take that! And that! And *that-and-that-and-that*!'
yelled Trundle, as he skipped and pranced among the
discomfited pirates, his sword a glimmering blur of
deadly steel. He never knew he had such courage in
him! Close by he could hear Esmeralda and Jack
causing chaos, Jack swinging the business end of
his rebec, Esmeralda brandishing the tiller-arm like
a bludgeon.

And then, almost before he knew it, Trundle

found himself standing on the foredeck of *The Gilded Lily*, panting for breath and gazing across the pirateless deck at his two companions.

'They're breaking off,' shouted Admiral Firwig. 'Look at them running! Joy in the morning, my lads. Run up the signal for victory!'

He was right. Many of the pirate ships were in flames, but those few that had escaped the attention of Captain Darkside's flame-throwers had already turned tail and were speeding away with every sail bulging. Unfortunately among those fleeing unharmed was *The Iron Pig*, and even as Trundle spotted it careening away from the battlefield, he heard a voice booming back through a megaphone.

'We're not done with you, Esmeralda Lightfoot!' roared the enraged Grizzletusk. 'We'll meet again, and then you and your little friends will be sorry you were ever born!'

Esmeralda looked at Trundle. 'I think we've upset the poor captain,' she said with a grin.

'Amery Wilde doesn't look too happy, either,' remarked Jack.

Of Wilde's six red wargalleons, three were in flames and two were running, and the sixth – *The Scarlet Scavenger* itself – had been boarded and subdued by Dolly Wideawake's Amazons. Captain Wilde was at that very moment being roped to his own mast with his dented silver helmet smashed down over his eyes.

'We can never thank you enough,' beamed Admiral Firwig, turning to Trundle, Esmeralda and Jack. 'You shall have a triumphal parade! A victory feast! Seven days of festivities! Statues commissioned for the Grand Square! Medals! Gold! The freedom of Swallowhaven!'

'Well, thanks very much,' smiled Trundle.

'That's very nice of you. But what we really need is for *The Thief in the Night* to be fully supplied with provisions so we can continue our quest.'

'What my dear sweet unworldly friend means,' said Esmeralda, sidling up to Trundle and putting a firm arm around his shoulders, 'is that we'd like the supplies *and* all that other stuff you said. If that's OK with you, of course.'

'No problem!' said the Admiral. He turned to a nearby officer. 'Signal all the fleet, my good fellow. Tell them we're heading for harbour!'

And so bright and cheerful signal flags were run up the mast of *The Gilded Lily* and the victorious windships of the Invincible Fleet of Swallowhaven headed for home.

It was not until quite a while later that anyone noticed the four ironclad windships of the steammoles of Hammerland had slipped quietly away.

*

'Well, the gifts of pure gold were my favourites,' said Esmeralda as *The Thief in the Night* sailed away through the empty skies that stretched far beyond the island of Swallowhaven. 'Pity it was all too heavy to take with us, but it'll make a nice little nest-egg once our quest is over.'

'I think I liked the feast best,' sighed Trundle, patting his stomach and remembering the tables of the Grand Banqueting Hall, piled so high with food and drink that you had to eat for an hour before you could even see who was sitting opposite you.

'I just adored the songs and the dances,' said Jack, lying in the bottom of the boat, tapping his long feet rhythmically against the mast and lazily bowing his rebec. 'It's a pity we couldn't stay for the full seven days of festivities, though.'

'One day was quite enough,' said Esmeralda.

'Another six days of feasting like that and we wouldn't have fitted in our clothes any more.'

'We wouldn't have even fitted in *The Thief in the Night*,' chortled Trundle. 'We'd have had to have found ourselves a bigger powerstone to keep us afloat.'

'Hello, hello, hello,' said Esmeralda, getting to her feet and peering off into the distance. 'What's that?'

'What?' asked Trundle.

'That there!'

'What where?'

'If you'd stir your lazy bones and look, you'd see *what where*,' Esmeralda retorted. 'It looks to me like a bit of a windship.'

Intrigued, Trundle and Jack got up and stared out over the prow of *The Thief in the Night*.

'By golly, I think you're right,' said Jack.

At first Trundle couldn't really make out the

tiny object at all. But then, as Esmeralda turned the tiller and they made a long slow curve towards the floating whatever-it-was, he began to realise what it was: a broken length of a windship's mainmast, complete with the crow's nest and the powerstone basket. And as they got closer, he also noticed the skinny and ragged shape of a hare, squatting on the basket and flapping his arms about as though he were swatting insects.

'The poor fellow,' said Jack. 'We must rescue him.'

'Ummm . . .' began Esmeralda. 'Well-ll-ll . . .'

Trundle looked at her. 'You're not seriously considering just leaving him there like that?' he protested. 'Not even you could be so heartless.'

'Of course not,' Esmeralda said indignantly. 'We could give him some food and water. You know, enough to keep him going till someone else comes along to rescue him. What do we do with him if we *do* pick him up? We're serious questers, Trundle, not a local ferry service.'

'But what if no one else *does* come along?' asked Jack. 'No! We have to bring him aboard – it's the only civilized thing to do.'

'And then what?' Esmeralda asked. 'We're heading off into uncharted regions. Where do we drop him off? Or are you suggesting we go all the way back to Swallowhaven with him?'

'I'm sure we'll find somewhere perfectly pleasant up ahead to put him ashore,' said Trundle.

Esmeralda shrugged. 'Very well, then. If you insist,' she said. 'But if this all goes pear-shaped, don't say I didn't warn you.'

As they moved cautiously closer to the floating chunk of mast, they could hear the flailing animal chattering away to himself.

'Flies and fleas, wasps and bees! Bite my nose and gnaw my knees! Without a *may I* or a *please*! Flies and fleas and wasps and bees!'

The Thief in the Night came up gently alongside the debris with its wretched babbling passenger. So far as they could tell, the air around the gibbering hare's head was quite empty of insects.

'Uh, hello there,' Trundle said amiably.

The scrawny figure became still, fixing him with a bulging and lunatic eye.

'Would ye have a cup of toenails for a poor lost mariner, me pretty bucko?' he asked in a high-pitched, screechy voice, his long ears twisting and untwisting above his head like propellers as he spoke.

'Not as such . . .' Trundle hesitantly replied.

Before anything more could be said, the hare made a flying leap on to *The Thief in the Night*, clutching at Trundle and sending him bumping on to his back on the bottom boards.

The tattered hare sat on him, staring around and grinning. 'Life begins at one o'clock!' he said, blinking his huge eyes at Esmeralda and Jack. 'Brandy for the parson's nose, if you please.'

Trundle gazed up at the manic hare. 'Are you entirely all right?' he asked in a squashed kind of voice. The newcomer was all skin and bones, but he was sitting full on Trundle's chest, which did make breathing a little difficult.

'Who be ye, me pretty bucko?' asked the hare, eyeing him again. 'I can see by yer snout you're as wise as a cuckoo's egg!' And so saying, he began to shriek with laughter, clutching at his knees and rocking back and forth on Trundle's chest while all poor Trundle could do was gurgle and splutter.

'Here, let me help you up,' Jack said kindly, lifting the skinny hare under his armpits and standing him on his feet. 'Welcome aboard *The Thief in the Night*.'

'Thief? Where thief? Who thief?' squeaked the hare, clutching at his ragged clothes and peering suspiciously about the skyboat. 'He'll get nothing from me, the dirty rotten burglar. A man's blackpowder pouch is his own private kingdom! I'll eat it first, so I will!'

'Calm down, my friend, there are no actual burglars aboard,' Jack explained. 'This skyboat is called *The Thief in the Night*.' He smiled and tapped at his own chest. 'I'm Jack Nimble, at your service. And that's Princess Esmeralda Lightfoot, the daughter of noble Roamany lineage. And the chappie sprawled on his back there is my very good friend Trundle Boldoak, a brave and bold adventurer.'

'Ishmael March is me name, me bright young button,' said the hare. 'Windship's cook, thirteen years before the mast.' He pointed to the floating debris. 'That there mast, to be exact.' He ran to the side of the skyboat and peered over the bow. 'But where's the rest of the windship gone? Where are me pots and me pans and me knives and me forks and me lemon squeezer and me asparagus tongs?'

'I think they're . . . um . . . gone,' said Esmeralda, spiralling one finger slowly downwards in a significant way. 'Sorry and all that. Have you been out here on your own for very long?'

'A while, your royal majestieness,' said Ishmael, blinking rapidly. 'I've been drifting adrift all on me tod, as it were, except for the buzzing fellers in me head, ever since the freakish firedrakes burned *The Gob Sprite* out from under me.'

'Hold on a minute,' said Trundle sitting up. '*The Gob Sprite*? That was the name of one of the pirate windships from the battle!'

Jack looked solemnly at the hare. 'Is that true?' he asked. 'Are you a pirate?'

Ishmael March held finger and thumb a fraction apart. 'A wee bit of a pirate, perhaps, on me mother's side,' he admitted. 'But not a fighting pirate, oh, my dear no. Windship's cook, that's me. Ishmael March, cook and . . . what was it they called me, now? It began with "L" and rhymed with *spoony*.'

'Loony?' Trundle offered.

Ishmael nodded and grinned. 'That'd be it!'

'A pirate!' said Esmeralda, folding her arms and giving Trundle and Jack a caustic look. 'We've taken a brain-addled pirate on board.' She snorted meaningfully. 'Great!'

'He looks harmless enough,' said Trundle. 'It's not like he's armed or anything.'

'That's what you think!' exclaimed Ishmael, whipping out a small potato peeler from his belt. 'Ready for any occasion, that's me! Bring on the spuds! I'll take their eyes out in a jiffy! I'll have their jackets from their backs, I will! That's old Ishmael!' He eyed each of them in turn. 'Thank 'ee mightily for rescuing me,' he cackled. 'Ye saved me from going mad, me salty herrings! Ye arrived in the nick of time to save old Ishmael from going stark mad!'

'I think we probably arrived just *after* the nick of time,' Esmeralda remarked under her breath.

'Well, now,' croaked Ishmael, 'one good turn deserves another. Show me to yer galley and I'll fix ye up a meal fit for a king!'

'We don't exactly have a galley, old chap,' said Jack. 'We've been pretty much living on sandwiches.'

'That's not fit fare for fighting folk!' declared Ishmael, rummaging through the barrels and boxes and bags of food they had picked up in Swallowhaven. 'Blackpowder and treacle,' he muttered shrilly to himself. 'With just a dash of brimstone! That'll wake him up! That'll blow sparks out o' his parson's nose!'

Trundle gazed for a few moments at the wriggling skinny back end of the hare as he dug through their provisions, then he looked from Esmeralda to Jack and back again.

'I suppose a cook would come in handy,' he said hopefully. 'Warm food would be nice – especially as we get further and further from the sun.'

Ishmael's head popped up, his ears whirling. 'Where be we a'going to, me brave hearties?' he asked.

'We're looking for the nest of the legendary glorious phoenix bird,' Jack told him.

'The legendary glorious phoenix bird, is it?' mused Ishmael, licking his lips. 'Sounds delicious! I could easily rustle you up a nice juicy slice of roast phoenix breast! Or phoenix drumsticks on a bed of lavender flowers and lettuce! Or phoenix nuggets in a blueberry sauce! That'll go down a treat, that will!'

'We're not going to *eat* him!' yelped Trundle. 'We're hoping he'll lead us to the Crown of Fire.'

'Is that so, now?' said Ishmael, tapping his lips thoughtfully. 'Well, have it your own way – but you might change your minds when I tell you a few of my top wild bird recipes! How does this strike a hungry ear, for instance? Imagine the phoenix bird spit-roasted over hot coals, basted with its own juices and served with a sauce of garlic, rosemary needles, sage leaves and juniper berries.'

'We are *not* eating him!' Esmeralda said decisively. 'Whatever next!' She rolled her eyes. 'But I suppose you're welcome to come along with us and do a bit of cooking if you like.' She looked meaningfully at Trundle and Jack. 'Now you're on board, you might as well make yourself useful.'

'You won't regret having old Ishmael as a crew mate,' chortled the hare. 'Just one bite of old Ishmael's cooking and your taste buds will love you for ever, you'll see!' He hunkered down and carried on rummaging through their provender. 'You won't regret it. Oh, no – you won't regret it for an instant!'

Trundle wasn't so sure.

6

Lord Slatterkin's Fancy

'Tis of the glorious phoenix bird, this story I

shall tell

In a nest of gold at the end of the world, this

wise old bird does dwell

The phoenix comes from fire and flame and

never saw a shell

Oh, the phoenix bright is a lovely sight, and keeps

his secret well!

87

Most marvellous and courteous bird, with

feathers red as flame

From Mithering to Jumper's Beat, afar has

spread his fame

Bring his lost feather to his nest with good

and noble aim

Oh, the phoenix bold in his nest of gold,

his secret will proclaim!

Trundle laughed and clapped as Jack stood at the prow of *The Thief in the Night*, singing lustily and sawing away at his rebec while Ishmael performed a wild and frantic dance amidships, his eyes popping and his ears revolving like windmill sails as he kicked up his heels with many a whoop and holler.

Esmeralda sat at the tiller, rubbing at her emptied plate with a final chunk of bread. 'Dinner and cabaret!' she sighed contentedly. 'Could any mortal animal ask for more?'

It was evening and the sky was turning a rich velvety blue, sewn with twinkling stars. Despite Trundle's reservations, Ishmael had proved himself a gifted and inventive chef. Rooting through the pile of provisions, he had unearthed a little stove on which to cook and a bag of coal for fuel and even a few saucepans and cooking utensils. Then, as they had sailed on, the most delicious and mouth-watering smells had begun to waft past the noses of the three adventurers.

As the daylight faded, they had come to a great dark mass of close-packed boulders and rocks. Checking the skycharts, they had learned that this immense reach of floating debris was known as Slatterkin's Reef. According to notes scribbled on the chart, the reef was an impassable labyrinth. But the eager phoenix feather thought differently, so it seemed

– because it pointed stiff and sure right into the middle of the tumbled mass of the reef.

It was at that point that Esmeralda suggested they moor for the night, have a good feed, get some much-needed kip, and then take a proper look at the reef first thing in the morning. No one had disagreed with this splendid plan, and so dinner had been organized, with musical entertainment to follow.

Trundle looked furtively around, then lifted his plate to his snout and gave it a long luxuriant licking. Bad manners, to be sure, but he blamed it on Ishmael's scrumptious cooking. It was irresistible!

A loud burp from Esmeralda proved that he was not the only one lacking proper decorum.

'Give us another tune, Jack,' Esmeralda shouted. 'And three cheers as well for Ishmael March, long may his saucepan steam!'

'Thank 'ee kindly, your majesticossity,' cackled

the hare. 'Old Ishmael he knows as thing or two about herbs and spices and soups and sauces, oh, yes, he does.' And he began to strut and cavort again, swinging himself around and around the mast and slapping his long feet together.

Laughing, Jack struck up a lively new tune and Esmeralda and Trundle clapped joyfully along. Had there been any creatures living this far from civilization they would have probably been surprised to hear laughter and singing and merry music sounding far into the starry night. And then, with the cooking fires doused and the little skyboat bobbing gently in the breeze, they would have heard the satisfied snoring of three sleeping beasts, along with the endless drowsy mutterings of a gusty, high-pitched voice.

'Blackpowder and treacle! Elbow grease and a long weight! Dance the hornpipe, Horatio! Blow it out his parson's nose! Kipper on the starboard cow! Trim

the mizzen, matey! Fifteen voles on a dead frog's chest. Avast behind! She's got a vast behind!'

'Ishmael?'

'Yes, your majestyness?'

'Shut *up*!'

'Well, I don't know,' Jack said, peering off into the dark expanse of Slatterkin's Reef. 'I can't see any obvious way through.'

They had not woken up quite as early as Esmeralda had suggested and were feeling a little blurry and drowsy from the late-night revels – all except Ishmael, it seemed, who leaped straight to his frying pan and began to prepare breakfast.

Slatterkin's Reef looked no less of an obstacle in the bright morning that it had the previous evening.

'Maybe we could go around it?' Trundle

suggested. 'Or over it? Or even under it? I mean, it can't go on for ever, can it?'

'No, not *for ever*, I don't suppose,' Esmeralda replied, staring at the skychart, which showed almost nothing but the black reef, across which were written the words: *Devoid of scientific interest*. 'But it could take us weeks to go all the way around, and that darned feather seems to want us to go straight through.'

She was right about that. The long red phoenix feather was aiming straight into the heart of the reef. Every now and then a shiver would run through it, as though it were impatient to be off.

'We are most definitely in the Devoids now,' sighed Jack. 'The only plan I can come up with is to follow the feather and hope for the best. There are plenty of channels and passages though the rocks, so far as I can make out – but whether they'll bring us safely out the other side, I wouldn't like to guess.'

'Breakfast up,' trilled Ishmael. 'Roamany toast for all, me hearties! It'll warm the cockles of yer hearts. Buckle up and sit ye down and get some of Ishmael's grub down yer necks! Things will look better in the morning.'

'We already *are* in the morning, Ishmael,' muttered Trundle as the cook handed him a plate. His face brightened as he sniffed the toasted cheese that Ishmael had provided.

Soon they were all sitting around, eating heartily and swigging buttermilk.

'You've got to give me the recipe for this, Ishmael, my friend!' exclaimed Jack, licking his lips.

'Treacle and blackpowder!' cackled the hare. 'With just a dash of brimstone. That'll wake him up – that'll blow sparks out o'his parson's nose!'

'That's not really what we're eating, is it?' Trundle asked.

The scraggy old hare just threw back his head and screeched with laughter.

After breakfast, they took *The Thief in the Night* into the reef, following the largest and straightest of the channels. The fact that there were no winds inside the maze of rocks only made things more difficult. Furling the sails, they took it in turns to work the treadles in the rear of the skyboat and so to drive it along with its little stern-mounted propeller.

The weather had gradually been getting more chilly as they travelled away from the sun, but now they were inside the shadowy reef, they finally began to feel properly cold. Warmer underwear was dug out of their provisions' hoard and this was topped up with the odd scarf and muffler and extra pair of woollen socks.

It was hard going with the treadles, made no easier by the fact that Ishmael was quite unable to help them. Within moments of him sitting on the treadle seat and starting to pump away with his legs, his long ungainly feet got tangled up and he ended up flat on his face in the bottom of the boat. Finally, they just sat him at the prow and let him shout useless instructions: 'Left hand down a bit – right hand up a bit – steady as she goes – there's a big rock – oooh, look, a boulder!' as they ploughed onwards.

Despite this, things seemed to be going reasonably well until, without any warning, the passageway corkscrewed, twisted, turned head over heels and tied itself into a knot, leaving them with no option but to head back and start all over again.

The next channel they followed widened and straightened, leading them deeper into the middle of the reef. Esmeralda was pedalling while Trundle and Jack stood at either bow, fending off the bigger chunks of rock.

'I think we're on to something here!' she puffed, her knees going up and down as the propeller whirred. 'At this rate we'll be through and out the other side before we know it!'

And then, as if to drive them all as mad as Ishmael, they came out into a small open area and saw at least twenty different channels opening up ahead of them.

'This is hopeless!' gasped Trundle. 'We'll never find our way through.'

'Look, we've been at it all morning.' Esmeralda rubbed her aching legs. 'Let's stop here for a spot of lunch and then consider our options.'

'A tip-top notion!' cackled Ishmael. 'And what say young Jack Nimble here lightens the load with a jolly tune or two to warm us all up and to get our toes a-tapping?'

'Whatever,' Esmeralda sighed, as the skyboat came to a halt.

Jack got out his rebec and started to play the tune of the phoenix song from the night before. It was rather jolly, and soon Esmeralda and Trundle were clapping along again and Ishmael was dancing on the spot as he peeled potatoes and boiled up some water on the stove.

'That's quite a dance you've got going there, Ishmael,' Jack said.

'It is that, to be sure,' said Ishmael. 'It's an old hornpipe me great-grand-pappy taught to me when I was just a nippy little nipper – it's always danced to that there melody you're playing, me lad.' He stirred some steaming sauce. 'It's called "Lord Slatterkin's Fancy".'

Trundle sat bolt upright. 'It's called *what*?'

'"Lord Slatterkin's Fancy,"' Ishmael repeated, his feet hopping and bopping and flipping and flapping as if they had a life of their own.

Jack's music came to a sudden halt and all three of them stared at Ishmael.

'Let me see if I've got this right,' Jack said. 'We're in a place called Slatterkin's Reef – and Ishmael here is dancing a dance called "Lord Slatterkin's Fancy".' He looked at Jack and Esmeralda. 'Anyone notice a strange coincidence here?'

'Coincidence be blowed!' said Esmeralda. 'It's the Fates, that's what this is! The Fates are showing us the way out of here. Ishmael, start the dance again from the beginning!' Her eyes gleamed. 'Watch closely, everyone. See exactly what he does.'

Ishmael began to prance about, chattering along to himself as he bounded around the skyboat. 'Five

hops left and round ye go, two hops right and dosey-
do! Three hops forward, one hop back, with a wiggle
and a waggle, go through the crack.'

Esmeralda stood up and stared at the channels.
'Fifth to the left,' she said, pointing at one of the dark
holes. 'That's the one! Trundle – man the treadles,
there's a good fellow. We're going to follow the steps
of this dance and I'll bet you every prickle on your
back that it'll lead us out of here before we know it!'

And so, with Ishmael March calling out the
steps as he danced, and Jack bowing the rebec and
Trundle pedalling for all he was worth and Esmeralda
yelling directions, *The Thief in the Night* made its way
through the maze of tunnels and causeways and
channels and passages.

The fifth channel curved around and ended
in a fork.

'Two hops right,' said Esmeralda, pointing

to the right-hand fork. 'That way!'

'What's a *dosey-do*?' asked Trundle.

The channel they were in tilted abruptly upwards then dropped down again.

'That is,' laughed Jack.

Suddenly they were confronted with one passageway that seemed to lead forward, and another that threatened to take them straight back to where they had started.

'One hop back,' said Trundle. 'We need to follow the tunnel that looks like the *wrong* one!'

'Now you're getting it,' said Esmeralda.

They headed into the channel. After a short distance, it began to zigzag violently from side to side and actually ended up turning over itself in a hairpin bend and sending them back the way they had wanted to go all along.

'Now that's what I call a wiggle and a waggle,'

said Esmeralda. 'Lawks, this is working!'

On and on they went, always choosing the tunnels and passageways suggested by the steps of Ishmael's crazy dance, until – quite suddenly it seemed – they pushed through a narrow gap between two huge boulders and burst out into bright afternoon sunlight.

Three hearty cheers echoed across the skies of the Sundered Lands.

They were through the reef!

The Magnificent
Phoenix Bird!

Trundle stopped pedalling and Jack stopped playing as *The Thief in the Night* floated clear of the great black reef.

Only Ishmael seemed unaware of their success. His arms and legs and ears worked furiously as he danced on, his eyes closed in concentration and his mouth spread in a wide, fixed toothy grin.

'Uh . . . Ishmael?' Esmeralda called to him.

'Swing your bottom through the air, leap out

into empty air . . .' panted the frantic hare.

'*Ishmael!*' Esmeralda hollered.

'Yes . . . your . . . highmostness . . .?'

'We're out of the reef. You can stop now.'

His limbs stopped flailing and his huge eyes popped open. 'Now that's a pity,' he said. 'I was just getting into me stride.' His eyes widened and he pointed over the prow. 'Drop me drawers and paint me backside blue! What's that?'

The other three had already spotted it. A solitary island was floating, lonely and forlorn in the distance – and rising from the middle of it was a tall, cone-shaped mountain.

'That, my friend,' declared Jack, 'is the land of the legendary phoenix bird!' He let out a relieved laugh. 'I'll eat my rebec and bow, rosin and all, if it isn't!'

Esmeralda wetted a finger and lifted it to test

the air. 'And there's a fine strong wind to take us there,' she said. 'Jack – unfurl the sails. We're away to journey's end!'

It wasn't long before the sail was up and *The Thief in the Night* was skimming jauntily through the clear cold skies. Trundle's elation began to dwindle a little as the lone island came closer. It looked a

miserable, desolate place: a barren land of grey rocks and pale, scrubby grasses and dead trees. The mountain reared upward, its wrinkled sides streaked with yellow stains. The

only sign of life anywhere was the yellowish smoke that clung about the high, broken-edged cone.

'Are we absolutely *sure* this is the right place?' Trundle wondered aloud. He couldn't quite imagine the glorious and marvellous phoenix bird choosing to live on such a glum and lifeless lump of rock.

'The feather seems to think so,' Jack replied.

Trundle looked over his shoulder. The feather was writhing and straining and pulling at the nail that held it as if desperate to get to the island.

'But it's so . . . so . . . *bleak*,' Trundle said.

'That's probably to keep tourists away,' suggested Esmeralda. 'I expect the phoenix was sick and tired of people constantly bothering him, telling him how beautiful and marvellous he was and asking for his autograph and so on. That's probably why he came here in the first place – to get away from all the razzmatazz.'

Jack nodded enthusiastically. 'I'm sure it'll look quite different inside the cone of the mountain. This is just camouflage. His nest will be utterly gorgeous and completely fabulous – just you wait and see!'

'Shall we fly straight up and in there, then?' asked Trundle.

'No, not at all,' said Jack. 'That would be most rude. We'll make landfall lower down the mountain and walk the rest of the way. We don't want to annoy him by plopping uninvited right in his lap, do we?'

'Especially not when we want him to tell us how to find the Crown of Fire,' added Esmeralda. 'Best keep on his good side, you know?'

The dismal island came gradually closer.

'Er, can anyone smell something . . . odd?' asked Trundle, sniffing the chill air. He wrinkled his snout. 'Something not particularly pleasant?'

'Don't look at me,' declared Ishmael. 'I didn't do it!'

'I think it's coming from the island,' said Trundle. He sniffed again. 'In fact – I'm sure it is. Pooh! What *is* it? Stinks like rotten eggs.'

'I think it's sulphur,' said Jack. 'Those yellowy clouds and those yellow streaks down the sides of the mountain are probably caused by escaping gases. It's not very nice, I'll grant you, but I don't think it's harmful.'

'Let's hope not,' said Esmeralda.

The unpleasant reek got gradually stronger as they sailed nearer to the island. By the time *The Thief in the Night* came in to settle lightly on the stony ground of a ridge about a third of the way up the mountain, the stench was almost overpowering.

Fortunately, Jack found a piece of cloth which he managed to tear into strips for them to tie over their muzzles and at least keep out the worst of the foul odour.

Trundle stood at the mast, using a knife to loosen the nail that was still holding the berserk feather as it struggled and fought to get free. As the nail came away, he just managed to snatch hold of the end of the feather before it zoomed off. Clutching it tightly, he stepped over the bow and joined the other three on the mountain. The ground felt oddly warm underfoot.

'All right, then,' said Esmeralda. 'Follow me, boys. And remember – when we meet the phoenix, be polite and well-behaved and sensible. Don't get all gushy and idiotic just because he's legendary and stuff. Oh, and Ishmael?'

'Yes, your worshipness?'

'Dial down the *loony* a tad, if you can, please. And no mention of wild bird recipes, got me?'

'Right you are!' chirruped Ishmael with a big

grin. 'You can trust old Ishmael to pack the giddy goat away with the monkeys in the kiddies' puzzle box, to be sure, you can!'

'Hmm,' said Esmeralda. 'If you say so. Trundle – keep an eye on him, will you? And if he looks like he's going to say something embarrassing, that strip of cloth over his nose will work a treat as a gag, if you catch my drift.'

And so they began the uphill trek.

It wasn't much fun. The mountain was steep and the ground underfoot was loose and slithery, and every now and then a stone or two would slip away under their feet and go rolling and rumbling down in a cloud of grey smoke.

Here and there, sad broken stumps of trees jutted out of the ground at curious angles, their leafless branches seeming to claw feebly at the sky. The occasional tuft of thin, wiry grass rustled in the slow-moving air, but there was no sight or sound of any animal life. As they climbed, they did their best to avoid the streaky smears of bubbling yellow sulphur that ran thick and stinky down the mountain's barren flanks.

If Esmeralda was right, and the phoenix had chosen this island to keep people away, then he'd certainly picked the perfect spot. In fact, the only enthusiastic member of the party was the feather. It became more and more excited as they climbed, until Trundle was only just able to keep hold of it.

'What's that noise?' asked Jack, pausing and lifting a paw. 'Do you hear it? An odd rumbling kind of noise.'

'Don't look at me,' said Ishmael. 'I didn't do it!'

Jack was right. Now that Trundle stopped and listened, he too was aware of the strange sound: a rolling, grumbling, wheezing noise that seemed to be coming from the top of the mountain. More than anything else, it reminded him of someone sawing logs with a blunt and rusty saw.

Grumble-rumble – wheeeeeeeze – grumble-rumble – wheeeeeeze.

There was a slow rhythm to the rumbling and grumbling that was very familiar, except that Trundle couldn't quite put his finger on it.

They carried on climbing. The curious noise grew louder and more insistent. The feather danced and cavorted in Trundle's paw.

At last, they were at the rim of the cone and the rhythmic refrain was all around them.

Grumble-rumble – wheeeeeeeze – grumble-rumble – wheeeeeeze.

Trundle stared down into the huge, cauldron-shaped hollow. He had been hoping – expecting, in fact – to see something unutterably wonderful, but all that seemed to be down there were swirling clouds of stinky yellow smoke that made his eyes water and tickled in his throat.

'Is this it?' asked Esmeralda, staring into the volcano.

'Um . . .' began Jack. 'Perhaps—'

He got no further before a gust of wind came prancing over the lip of the volcano and dived down inside, stirring the yellow clouds and scattering them so that suddenly the four travellers had a much clearer view.

And what they saw quite took their breath away.

It was the phoenix nest!

But it was nothing like they had been expecting. Far from being marvellous and glorious, the nest was a huge ruinous heap of spiky briars and thorny brambles, all tangled up together in the bottom of the crater. And lying curled up on its side in the middle of the whole ugly mess was the most gigantic, mangy, decrepit, wrinkled old bird imaginable, with drool running from its open beak and horrid yellow crusty gunk around its screwed-up eyes.

And even as they stood gaping at the unbelievable sight, a rasping sound blasted from the phoenix's rear end. 'Pardon me,' muttered the phoenix in a sleepy, cracked old voice as a wave of foul air wafted up towards them.

'Granted!' chortled Ishmael.

8

Blackpowder and Treacle

Esmeralda turned very slowly to Jack. 'That,' she began heavily, as if she were having trouble putting her feelings into words, 'that thing . . . that thing down there . . .' her voice rose to a shriek, '. . . *that thing down there is your marvellous and beautiful phoenix bird?*'

Another loud report sounded from the sleeping bird's rear end.

'Beg pardon,' it croaked.

'Granted again,' cackled Ishmael. 'A person must strain his greens when the wind blows from the north.'

Trundle clapped his paw to his nose as the gust of evil air reached them.

Jack blinked down at the bird. 'You can't blame me for this!' he said rapidly. 'I'm as disappointed as the rest of you. Blame the people who made up the legend! Blame the songwriters! I was just repeating what I was told. Who would have expected it to look like *that*? Not me! It's a swizz, that's what it is. It's chicanery and distortion and . . . and . . . downright fibbing! We should take legal action. We should sue someone.' His voice became a miserable wail. 'It's not my fault!'

For a few moments, no one said anything.

'We are quite certain this is *the* phoenix, are we?' Trundle asked at last.

'What else could it be?' Esmeralda replied. 'Percy told us the legends say the phoenix lives in a volcano at the end of the world. This is a volcano, sure enough, and I'm guessing we're pretty much at the far end of the Sundered Lands.'

'And apart from where it's gone grey, or its feathers have fallen out, its plumage is the same colour as the feather that brought us here,' Jack added. 'I'm sorry, but I don't think there can be any doubt about it. That mangy old wreck down there is the phoenix we've been searching for.'

'Lawks a mussy,' breathed Esmeralda. 'Who'd a'thought it?'

'Blimey,' groaned Trundle. 'Talk about a letdown!'

'There's not much meat on him for roasting, the poor old codger,' said Ishmael. 'But on the bright side, he'll boil up a treat for stock, if we can find a big enough pot.'

'Be quiet, Ishmael, we're *still* not eating him,' said Esmeralda. Her voice became quite matter-of-fact, and she rubbed her paws together briskly. 'Well, then, I suppose we'd better send someone down there to talk to him. We need him to tell us where to find the Crown of Fire, don't forget.' She looked from Jack to Trundle. 'Any volunteers?'

Prrrrrrrrrrrph! sounded from the phoenix, followed by a muttered, 'Beg pardon.'

'Lummee!' groaned Jack, clutching his nose. 'Down there? I don't think so.'

'Its not fair, just one of us having to go down,' said Trundle. 'We should all go.'

'Last one down's a pickled pilchard!' chortled Ishmael, jumping over the lip of the wide cauldron and prancing down its steep slope towards the nest.

'Quick, after him!' said Esmeralda. 'For all we

know he'll start trussing the phoenix up for the oven!'

Trundle and Jack and Esmeralda scrambled down in Ishmael's cavorting wake. It wasn't till they had slithered and slid and scrabbled and scrobbled all the way down to the twisted and knotted nest that they got a real impression of the full size of the ancient bird. They peered up at the phoenix through the tangled brambles.

'It's as big as a dragon!' gasped Jack.

'Bigger,' breathed Esmeralda.

'I've never seen a dragon,' offered Trundle. 'Particularly, big, are they?'

'Fairly big,' said Jack. He cocked a thumb at the phoenix. 'About *that* big, generally speaking.'

The huge snoring bird reared up above them, as high as the roof of Trundle's little cottage back in Port Shiverstones, and at least twice as wide. From up close, he looked even more mangy and wrinkly and wretched than before.

Ishmael was already clambering through the spiky nest, giggling to himself and muttering about roasting dishes and basting spoons.

Rrrrrrrpppppph! came a fresh report from the huge bird.

''Scuse me . . .' he muttered drowsily. 'Must apologize . . .'

'Pardon me for being rude,' burbled Ishmael. 'It was not me it, was my food, a message came right from my heart, it were no burp, it were –'

'Enough poetry, I think, Ishmael,' Esmeralda called. She gave her companions a hollow-eyed look. 'Come on, let's get this over with. We need to wake him up somehow!'

Very cautiously, they clambered in Ishmael's wake through the thorny and spiky web of the nest. A spike got itself jammed in Trundle's jacket and it took all three of them to pull him loose. Jack was stabbed in the toe by a needle-sharp thorn and he took some time out to hop about and swear before he felt able to continue. But at last they made their way through and met up again with Ishmael at the beak-end of the enormous bird.

Trundle could hardly bring himself to look at the seedy and haggard old phoenix. Thick drool seeped from the gaping beak and his abominable breath was nearly as bad as the smells that came from his other end. Then there was the crusty yellow gunk smeared all around his wrinkly old eyes, not to mention the bald patches where withered skin showed grey and saggy on his neck and head and chest. And all the while they stood there, his incessant snoring filled the air and made the ground tremble under their feet.

'Someone wake him up, then!' shouted Esmeralda over the deafening din.

'How?' yelled Jack.

'Poke him, or something,' Esmeralda suggested. 'Shout in his ear!'

'Trundle, you're good at that sort of thing,' said Jack. 'Go for it, lad!'

'What do you mean, *I'm* good at that sort of thing?' exclaimed Trundle. 'I'm nothing of the sort.'

'Hands up for Trundle waking the phoenix!' shouted Esmeralda.

The hands of Jack, Esmeralda and Ishmael shot into the air.

'Oh, thanks a bunch!' said Trundle, with heavy irony. 'Very fair, I call that!' But there was no point in arguing. He might just as well get on with it. After all, he thought, the sooner we get what we came for, the sooner we can get away from here.

He stepped gingerly up to the side of the bird's head. 'Hoy!' he yelled into his feathery ear. 'Hoy! Phoenix! Wakey-wakey!'

The phoenix made no response.

Trundle leaned in closer, cupping his paws around his mouth. '*Hoy!*' he bellowed. '*Hoy-oy-oy!* Wake up, you mangy old wreck!'

'Trundle!' Esmeralda called anxiously. 'Don't upset him!'

'Upset him?' said Trundle. 'How can I do that? He can't hear a thing. He's probably stone deaf on top of everything else.'

'Give him a good hard nudge,' suggested Jack. 'That might do the trick.'

Trundle picked his way down the vast bird. He braced himself and jabbed a shoulder into the phoenix's belly.

Phrrrrttt!

'Manners!' mumbled the phoenix.

'Crikey!' gasped Trundle, grabbing his snout in both hands. 'Save us! I'm being gassed!'

'Where ere ye go, by land or sea, ye must always let yer wind go free!' cackled Ishmael, prancing from foot to foot. 'That's what me great-grand-pappy taught to me!'

Shaking her head, Esmeralda clambered up to the bird's head. 'Excuse me, Mr Phoenix Bird!' she bellowed at the top of her voice. 'Wake up now, there's a good fellow!'

She paused, her fists on her hips, her eyes narrowing determinedly.

'*Fire!*' she hollered. '*The nest's on fire!* Every bird for himself!'

Grumble-rumble – wheeeeeeeze – grumble-rumble – wheeeeeeze.

She turned her back to the bird, throwing her

arms up. 'Well, that's me done! Anyone else got any bright ideas? Ishmael, will you please shut up for a minute, I can't hear myself think above his snoring and your endless prattle!'

Trundle cocked an ear towards the dancing pirate. He was talking his usual nonsense – but it suddenly occurred to Trundle to pay better attention to Ishmael's ramblings.

'Blackpowder and treacle – with just a dash of brimstone. That'll wake him up – that'll blow sparks out o'his parson's nose!'

Trundle's eyes widened. He stumbled back to the others in sudden excitement. 'Listen to Ishmael!' he told them.

They listened.

'He's always saying that,' Esmeralda retorted. 'He's potty. So what's new?'

'But what if it means something?' Trundle

insisted. 'Listen again.'

'Blackpowder and treacle – with just a dash of brimstone. That'll wake him up – that'll blow sparks out o'his parson's nose!'

Jack's eyes widened. 'Trundle, you're a complete genius! That's not nonsense at all – it's a recipe for a potion to wake someone up.'

'Not just *someone*,' said Trundle. 'The phoenix!' He looked at Esmeralda. 'You're always going on about the Fates being on our side. Well, I think you're right. The Fates sent Ishmael to us, and Ishmael is giving us the very method we need to wake this stinky old ruin up!'

'There's treacle on *The Thief in the Night*,' said Jack. He turned to Ishmael. 'Hey, have you got any blackpowder on you, old chap?'

'Surely I do,' cried Ishmael, pulling a small leather pouch from inside his raggedy shirt. 'A pirate

must keep his powder close and dry, or the cannon
go quiet and the balls won't fly.'

'Good, good,' said Esmeralda, Trundle's
enthusiasm reflected in her gleaming eyes. 'So,
we've got treacle and blackpowder. But what
about brimstone? I don't even know what
brimstone is.'

'Whee-yoop!' shrieked Jack. 'I do! *I do!*
It's sulphur! Brimstone is another name for sulphur,
and the outer slopes of this mountain are covered
in the stuff! All we need to do is gather some in a
pot, mix it with treacle and some of
Ishmael's blackpowder, and – hey
presto – instant wake-up potion!'

'And once the phoenix
is awake, we give him back
his feather,' said Trundle.

'And he tells us

where to find the Crown of Fire,' whooped Esmeralda. 'Job done!'

Brrrrrph!

'Who did that?' mumbled the phoenix.

'You did, you foul old fowl!' chortled Ishmael.

9

Riddles

They were on the outer slopes of the mountain. Jack had clambered all the way back to *The Thief in the Night* and returned with a jar of treacle, a medium-sized saucepan and a large spoon.

Wincing and clutching his nose with one paw, Trundle had been *volunteered* to go and fetch some of the nasty yellowy sulphur stuff. He came back with a brimming spoonful, holding it at arm's length. The others backed away as he emptied the thick stinking goop into the saucepan.

'So?' he asked. 'What are the proportions of the mixture?' He looked at Ishmael. 'You know, the recipe. How much treacle to how much brimstone and so on.'

'Just lob the stuff in, Trun,' said Esmeralda, from a safe distance. 'I don't think you'll need to be too precise.'

Shrugging, Trundle unscrewed the lid from the jar of treacle and poured in a few thick dollops on top of the sulphur brimstone. There was a blubbery sort of blooping noise from within the saucepan and some steam rose up.

Next, Trundle opened the pouch of blackpowder and poured its contents into the saucepan. The mixture hissed and bubbled and smoked.

'Stir it nicely,' suggested Esmeralda.

'I don't know why *I* have to do it all,' Trundle

remarked, as he poked at the smelly mess in the saucepan with the spoon.

'Because there's no point in all of us being at risk, is there?' Esmeralda explained.

'At risk?' exclaimed Trundle. 'At risk of *what*?'

'Nothing at all,' Esmeralda said reassuringly. 'Don't make such a fuss. Now mix it all up like the good fellow you are, and then we can get busy.'

'Well, it had better work, that's all I can say,' mumbled Trundle as he attacked the oozing goo with the spoon. 'And the next time any of us has to do something totally revolting – it's not going to be me!'

'No, of *course* not,' said Esmeralda, far too quickly.

With the wake-up potion mixed, Trundle picked up the saucepan by the very tip of its handle and carried it back up the mountain.

'Where exactly did you hear about this potion?'

Jack asked Ishmael as they followed Trundle at a discreet distance.

'I learned it at me great-grand-pappy's knee, so I did,' said Ishmael. 'And he learned it at *his* great-grand-pappy's knee. And *his* great-grand-pappy learned it from *his* great-grand-pappy.' As he spoke, his voice got gradually faster. 'And his great-grand-pappy learned it from his great-grand-pappy. And-his-great-grand-pappy-learned-it-from-his-great-grand-pappy. *Andhisgreatgrandpappylearnedit . . .*'

'Enough with the great-grand-pappies!' exploded Esmeralda. 'Let's just assume it's been in your family for a while, eh?'

'It surely has, your ladyshippiness,' said Ishmael. 'It surely has.'

Grumbling to himself, Trundle began the descent to the broken-down old nest and the even more broken-down old bird.

'How do I get lumbered with these jobs?' he muttered under his breath. 'Have I got *doormat* tattooed on my forehead, or something? Have I got *gullible twit* stamped on my snout?'

'What are you going on about, Trundle?' called Esmeralda from several paces behind.

'Nothing!' said Trundle. 'I'm just remarking on how much *fun* it is to be the one with the saucepan.'

'Good for you!'

'Grmph!'

Trundle clambered through the nest, careful not to allow the saucepan to be knocked out of his paw by the thorns and briars.

He arrived at the top end of the phoenix, and looked back to see the other three peering at him through the jagged mesh of branches and twigs.

'Be careful, Trundle!' Esmeralda called. 'He might be a bit grumpy at first. You know what

old people can be like if they're woken up from a deep sleep.'

'Thanks!' snorted Trundle. 'I'll bear it in mind.'

He turned to the phoenix. Taking a deep, deep breath, he leaned forward and tipped the saucepan over above the bird's open beak. The thick blobby mixture came flopping out and landed with a squelchy splat on the sleeping bird's tongue.

Trundle jumped back.

'Anything happening?' called Jack, after a few moments.

'Not a lot,' said Trundle.

'Ishmael, if you've been messing us about—' began Esmeralda.

'Wait!' yowled Trundle, taking another step back. The huge beak had closed and opened and closed again and a *mnyumm-mnyummm-mnyummm* noise was coming from the phoenix.

'Very tasty,' the bird mumbled. 'Very sweet . . .'

And then, with a suddenness that knocked Trundle on to his backside, the eyes of the huge bird snapped open, steam came hissing from his nostrils and ears and he sat bolt upright with his neck stretched up and a startled and stunned look on his face.

A second later, the beak opened and smoke gushed out. '*Gahhhh!*' gasped the phoenix, cross-eyed. '*Gahhh-gugggg-gahhhh!*'

'Uh, hello there!' called Trundle, getting back onto his feet.

'Who? What? Where? Why? How?' gabbled the phoenix, his head twisting back and forth on his long scraggy neck.

'Yoo-hoo! Down here,' said Trundle, waving.

The beak dropped and the bloodshot eyes

uncrossed and the phoenix
fixed Trundle with
a terrible gaze.

'You'd
better have
my tail-feather
with you, boy,'
croaked the ancient
bird, 'or I'll want to know
the reason why!'

'Yes! Yes, I do,'
said Trundle, pulling the
feather out from inside
his jacket, where he'd
tucked it again for
safekeeping. 'Look! It's
right here.'

The long neck

bent and the head stooped down so that Trundle found himself snout-to-beak with the bad-tempered bird.

'Hrumph, lucky for you!' said the phoenix. 'So – what kept you? Have you got any idea of how long I've been sitting around waiting for you to arrive? Do you, eh? Do you?'

'Well, no,' Trundle admitted. 'But it's been a while, I would imagine.'

'A *while?*' The phoenix almost choked with indignation. 'It's been two thousand years, you young whippersnapper! Two thousand years!' And so saying, he snapped his beak closed on the feather and tore it out of Trundle's paw.

Trundle became aware of Esmeralda and the others at his side. They waited in polite silence while the phoenix twisted himself around with a few arthritic groans and gasps, finally managing to insert the lost feather into the raggy plumage close to his rear parts.

He turned back to them. 'Well, now,' he said in a less grumpy tone, 'what can I do for you? I take it you haven't come all this way just out of the kindness of your hearts.'

'You are quite correct, oh beautiful and puissant phoenix,' said Esmeralda.

'*Beautiful?*' whispered Trundle, staring at her in disbelief.

'Work with me, here, Trun,' Esmeralda hissed out of the corner of her mouth. 'Flattery never hurts!'

'We have travelled far through the endless blue skies of the Sundered Lands,' said Jack. 'Seeking for the lost Fiery Crown of the Badger Lords of Old. Could it be possible that in your glory and wisdom, you might be able to help us in our noble quest, oh marvellous and awe-inspiring phoenix?'

'I might,' said the phoenix, lifting a wing and giving himself a quick grooming-type peck about

under there. 'But first you must answer me this riddle.'
He coughed and his eyes turned skywards as if he was
trying to remember something. 'Ah, yes. That's it.' His
voice rose into a singsong croak. 'Light as a feather,
there's nothing to it. But the strongest of creatures
cannot hold it for more than a minute. What is it?'

'I'm not much good with riddles,' said
Esmeralda.

Trundle grinned. 'But I am,' he said, the merest
hint of smugness coming into his voice. 'The answer is
"breath",' he said, looking up at the phoenix. 'Am I
right or am I right?'

'Perfectly right,' said the phoenix. 'Well done.'

'I would have got it eventually,' said
Esmeralda. 'So? Oh, beauteous and delightful phoenix,
can you tell us now where we will find—'

'Which side of a phoenix has the most
feathers?' asked the phoenix.

'I'm sorry?' said a puzzled Esmeralda.

'Answer the riddle,' said the phoenix.

Esmeralda frowned. 'The top side?' she offered.

No,' croaked the phoenix. 'Only two tries left.'

'You never told us there was a limit on how many tries we could have!' said Esmeralda.

'You never asked,' replied the phoenix. 'Rules is rules. Take it or leave it.'

'And if we don't guess right in the next two goes?' asked Jack.

'Then you can just turn around and go back where you came from, for all I care,' said the phoenix. 'I don't give my secret away to the first simpleton who turns up here with a feather in its paw, you know. I do have my standards.'

'The front side!' exclaimed Esmeralda.

'No!'

'Esmeralda, stop guessing,' hissed Trundle.

'Give me a moment to think.'

'I'll count down from ten,' announced the phoenix. 'Ten. Nine. Eight . . .'

'The outside!' blurted Trundle. 'The outside of a phoenix has the most feathers.'

'Cor-r-r-r-rect,' croaked the bird. He fixed Trundle with a yellowy and bloodshot eye. 'You're a smart one, and that's a fact! What must be broken before it can be used?'

'Oh, for heaven's sake,' groaned Esmeralda.

'An egg!' said Trundle with sudden inspiration.

'Quite right,' said the phoenix, nodding approvingly. 'Now then. What bird is always with you when you eat?'

'The very spotty chocolate-gull,' chimed Ishmael.

'No such creature,' declared the phoenix. 'Two more chances!'

'The spindle-shanked purple-plumed double-breasted throat-warbler!' yelled Ishmael.

'Stop making birds up, you idiot!' shouted Esmeralda.

'Just trying to help,' said Ishmael. 'What about the ginger-headed, bow-legged . . .'

'The swallow!' yelled Trundle. 'The swallow! The swallow! *The swallow!*'

'Yes,' replied the phoenix. 'And yes, and yes, and *yes*!'

'Are we done now with the bird riddles?' asked Esmeralda.

'Yes,' said the phoenix. 'Yes, you are done with the bird riddles.' He stretched his long neck and his feathers bristled. 'And now for the final test. Riddle me this!

My first is never in pot, but always in pail

My second is in tool, but never in tail

My third is in log, but isn't in leg

My fourth is in nail, but nowise in ale,

My last is in yolk, but never in egg.

What am I?'

'Tricky,' said Trundle. He looked at his companions. 'I was never very good at this kind of thing.'

'Don't let us down now, Trundle,' said Esmeralda. 'Think!'

'I am thinking,' said Trundle. 'It isn't helping.'

'Well, let's *all* think about it, then,' said Jack. 'What never goes in a pot, but is always found in a pail?'

'It's me!' shouted Ishmael. 'Me! Me! Me!'

'I don't think *you* can be the answer, Ishmael,' said Jack.

'I am, too!' hooted Ishmael, hopping from foot

to foot. 'Old Ishmael, he knows! Old Ishmael is a strange bird!'

'Cut it out, Ishmael,' Trundle said crossly. 'I can't think with you yelling. I really don't think the riddle has anything to do with things that go into actual pots and pails. It's probably more to do with the letters used in the words.'

'Then what's the answer?' asked Jack.

'I'm not sure . . .' moaned Trundle.

'Oh, I am so totally sick of all this nonsense!' hollered Esmeralda, stamping her foot. She jammed her fist on her hips and turned to the phoenix, every prickle on her body quivering with frustration and annoyance. 'Now look here, Mr Phoenix, we came all the way here – battling pirates and navigating through Slatterkin's Reef, I might add – with the specific purpose of giving you back your feather so you could tell us your secret.'

'Esmeralda?' murmured Trundle, plucking at her sleeve. 'It might not be wise to yell at him.'

'Be quiet a moment, Trun,' said Esmeralda. 'I'm busy yelling right now.' She glared up at the bemused-looking bird. 'So – enough with the riddles and the brain-teasers and the puzzles. I don't care what your first is in, mister! Or your second, or, in fact, your third, fourth and fifth. You want to know what you are? I'll tell you what you are. You are a *loony*!'

'Correct,' croaked the phoenix. 'Loony is the answer.'

'He's right, you know,' said Trundle. 'Loony *is* the answer. Well, I never! Ishmael had it right all along.'

'So, *now* will you tell us where the Crown of Fire can be found?' asked Esmeralda.

'Not just yet,' said the phoenix.

'Oh, strike me pink and blue!' raged Esmeralda.

'What now? Card tricks? A spelling bee?'

The phoenix lifted its head to the full extent of its threadbare neck and spoke in an increasingly dramatic voice. 'The secret of the glorious phoenix bird will only . . . be . . . revealed . . . when . . .' He paused.

'Yes?' chorused Jack and Esmeralda and Trundle.

'. . . whe-en . . .'

'Yes – *when*?' they all yelled.

'When I die!' finished the phoenix.

An awkward silence descended within the cone of the volcano.

'Oh,' said Jack. 'I see.'

There was another long pause.

'And, if you don't mind us asking,' Esmeralda began. 'Would you have any idea of when that might be?'

'Esmeralda!' whispered Trundle. 'You can't ask a question like that.'

The phoenix frowned at her, as though thinking hard. 'Well,' he said, narrowing his eyes. 'I'd say . . . it should be . . . some time . . . about . . . *now*!'

Even as the final word came out of his beak, there was a tremendous roaring noise and a blaze of blinding red fire filled the entire crater, lifting the four animals right off their feet and sending them whirling through the air like dandelion seeds.

Cold Blue
Flames

Soaring through the air like a Swallowhaven swallow,

Trundle came in to land upside down and part way up

the crater of the volcano.

Wallop!

'Ow!' Blinking and coughing, he slid slowly

downwards. 'Ow! Ouch! Ow-ow-ow!'

On either side, he could hear the gasping and

groaning of his companions. They'd fared no better

than he had. The titanic explosion set off by the

dying phoenix had sent all four of them crashing

through the nest and splatted them against the

wall of the crater like four badly-flung

omelettes.

It was a few moments before the white smoke

cleared and Trundle and the others managed to get

themselves upright and on their feet and were

able to see the full effects of the blast.

'Didn't I tell ye it would

blow smoke out o'his parson's

nose!' croaked Ishmael,

rubbing dust out of his rolling

eyes. 'Didn't old Ishmael

tell 'ee?'

'He's gone,'

gasped Trundle.

'Completely gone!'

'He's dead,'

added Jack. 'The poor old fellow.'

'But what a way to go!' said Esmeralda.

The straggly nest had been all but blown to pieces as the phoenix expired. And in the place where the old bird had been sitting, there was now nothing but a neat pile of grey ash, shrouded in wisps and strands of white smoke.

'That's what I call a death scene,' said Esmeralda, straightening her clothes. 'You had to admit, the old guy knew how to make an exit!'

'But he didn't tell us the secret!' groaned Trundle. 'He . . . um . . . *went off* before he told us where we could find the Crown of Fire.'

'I'm not so sure he did,' said Jack. He took a step forwards. 'What's *that*?'

Trundle looked.

There was something in the middle of the heap of ash. Something small and flickery and blue.

'It can't be . . .' said Esmeralda in disbelief.

'It is!' said Jack.

'It's the Crown of Fire!' gasped Trundle. He ran forward, scattering pieces of blasted nest to either side. 'Ooh! Ow!' he squeaked, as his feet made contact with the hot ash. He stood hopping from foot to foot at the outer margins of the ash-heap.

He could see the crown clearly now. It was quite exquisite – a tall elegant shape with jagged points like the shards of a broken eggshell. It flickered and danced like blue fire trapped in a vessel of glass.

Esmeralda and Jack arrived at his side.

'The Crown of Fire!' breathed Jack. 'It's lovely! Absolutely gorgeous!'

'It's rather more fiery than I had expected,' said Esmeralda. She looked at them. 'Anyone got any bright ideas as to how we actually transport this thing?'

'Iron tongs to pick it up,' suggested Jack. 'And

an insulated, fire-proof box to keep it in.'

Esmeralda eyed him. 'So we have those things aboard the *Thief in the Night*?' she asked. 'Because if we do, I haven't spotted them.'

'Um,' said Jack.

'What a pretty gewgaw, me hearties!' chortled Ishmael, his paws clutched together under his chin and his ears spinning. 'What a lovely, toasty thing to keep a fellow's head warm in these chilly climes!'

And so saying, he went prancing into the ashes, kicking up fine white dust as he went.

'Ishmael, no!' shrieked Esmeralda. 'You'll be burned to a crisp!'

But Ishmael ignored her. He danced across the ash-heap and began to leap and cavort around the flickering blue crown, sending the ash billowing up all around him.

'Don't touch it!' called Trundle. 'Be sensible!'

Ishmael bent down and picked up the crown. Trundle winced, not wanting to watch.

'I'm the king of the ca-astle, and you're all dirty ra-ascals!' came Ishmael's crazy voice.

Trundle opened his eyes. Ishmael had put the fiery crown on his head. It was rather too big for him – if not for his ears, it would probably have been dangling around his neck. But it was clearly not burning him. He was tripping the light fantastic in the ash, singing and chuckling and snapping his fingers as he danced.

'Isn't it rather hot?' called Jack.

'Not at all, not at all,' cackled Ishmael. 'Warm as woolly mittens, it is – I can feel it doing me head the world o'good. I can feel it warming up the old brain like soup in a kettle!'

'Amazing!' said Esmeralda.

Quite suddenly, Ishmael stopped dancing. A

glazed look came over his bulging eyes and he began to speak in a strange shrill voice.

'This clue you have found in the phoenix bird's fire
You must seek for the Crown of Ice in the
land of Spyre!'

Then, a moment later, Ishmael shook himself all over and started dancing and singing again as if nothing had happened.

'Did you hear that?' said Esmeralda. 'We've not only found the Crown of Fire, but we've just been given a clue to help us with the next one!'

'The land of Spyre?' puzzled Trundle. 'I've never heard of it.'

'I have,' said Jack. 'It's an odd place, to be sure. Full of mystery and mysticism, so the stories say. And it's a curious shape, too – like an elongated teardrop with jungles at one end and snowy mountains at the other. And in the middle . . .'

'Yes?' prompted Trundle. 'In the middle?'

Jack put a finger to the side of his muzzle.

'Marvellous secrets!' he whispered with a slow wink.

'Such as?' asked Esmeralda.

Jack shrugged. 'I don't know, they're secret.'

Ishmael came gambolling through the ash.

'We're off to Spyre, yo ho, yo ho!' he sang. 'We're off to Spyre, in the snow, in the snow!'

They stared after him for a few moments as he went scrambling up the mountainside with the flaring and fluttering Crown of Fire still on his head.

'Follow that pirate!' said Esmeralda.

It took a while for them to persuade Ishmael to part with the crown, but in the end he agreed to take it off. It was an extraordinary, wonderful thing, quite solid to the touch, smooth and still a little warm – like sun-heated glass – its blue fires flickering and flaring.

They found a box with a lid that had once held windship's biscuits. The crown fitted perfectly in there. And so, with everyone aboard, and with Jack at the boom and Esmeralda at the tiller, *The Thief in the Night* lifted off from the mountainside and sailed back towards Slatterkin's Reef.

They hoped that the Fates would guide them through the reef again – and if the Fates proved less than totally helpful, they could always get Ishmael to dance Slatterkin's Folly backwards.

'I do feel a bit sad about the phoenix, though,' remarked Trundle as they sped away from the lonesome island. 'I know he was old and curmudgeonly and all that, but it's a shame he had to die.'

'If you gotta go, you gotta go, Trundle,' said

Esmeralda. 'He was at least a couple of thousand years old, don't forget.'

'All the same,' sighed Trundle.

'Fetch hot water and plenty of towels!' screeched Ishmael, staring back the way they had come. 'It's on its way!'

'What is?' asked Jack.

'The new-born chicklet!' shrieked Ishmael. 'Do ye not know the legend? The phoenix rises from the ashes of its own funeral pyre, so it does!' His voice rose to a whoop. 'Happy birthday and many returns!'

As he spoke, a beam of bright red light came shooting up out of the mountain's cone, bathing the entire sky with a ruby glow. And rising up within the beam of rosy light, was a truly magnificent young phoenix bird! Its glorious wings spread out as wide as the crater's rim, radiant now in shining scarlet plumage. Its noble head lifted majestically on a long sinuous neck and its eyes shone like twin suns.

'Oh . . . wow . . .' gasped Trundle, shading his eyes from the glorious radiance.

Up and up the newborn phoenix rose, revealing jewelled claws and a long sweeping red tail. It flapped its scarlet wings, its eyes filled with light and joy as its beak stretched wide open.

'Good luck!' called the beautiful bird, its voice ringing out like a peal of golden bells. 'Good luck and thank you!'

And with that, the wonderful creature sank back down into the cone of the volcano and the ruby light faded.

'Well,' breathed Trundle. 'Now there's a bird who knows how to make an *entrance*!'

ALLAN FREWIN JONES
AND GARY CHALK

Allan was born under the kitchen floor of a derelict house in south-east London. At the age of nine, he inherited a typewriter and, for want of anything better to do, began to write stories. He had his first book published at the age of one hundred and three; lots more followed. He has a German wife, an English cat and a collection of old Beano annuals and lives in the same derelict house where he grew up.

Gary was born under a bush and brought up by a family of weasels. He was hopeless in school except for art, English and history, in which he weasely came top of the class. After working as a teacher for a while, he became an illustrator, and drew the pictures for many of the Redwall books. He lives with his wife in a farmhouse in the French countryside, working in a huge attic.

Read on for the thrilling continuation in:

The Ice Gate of Spyre

'Can I wear the crown again yet?' asked Ishmael, twisting his ears between his paws and looking at his three companions with big, mournful eyes.

'No,' Esmeralda replied, for the tenth time. 'The Crown of Fire is staying safe and sound in its biscuit tin.'

Trundle gazed sympathetically at the loony ship's cook. Ishmael seemed so sad, sitting there forlornly in the narrow prow of *The Thief in the Night*.

'Never you mind, old pal,' said Jack, perching on the skyboat's rail at Ishmael's side and lightly running his bow across the strings of his rebec. 'Let me cheer you up with a merry ditty.'

'Rattle me bones and strain me gravy,' sighed Ishmael, his long head between his paws. 'Even an oyster has his wheelbarrow, and that's a fact!'

Trundle did feel sorry for the poor old chap. It wasn't so very long ago that the loopy hare had been strutting around in the ruins of the phoenix nest, the beautiful fiery crown jammed on to his head, spouting out clues for the next stage of their quest.

'This clue you have found in the phoenix bird's fire
You must seek for the Crown of Ice in the land
of Spyre!'

Trundle had never heard of Spyre, but Jack had a

pretty good idea of how to get there. The carefree musician had been everywhere and seen everything. Sometimes Trundle felt quite inadequate, remembering his quiet, dull, little life on the windswept flats of Shiverstones, with its acres and acres of dismal, depressing cabbages. Although his life hardly lacked for excitement since he had met up with Esmeralda!

'Here's a little song I've written about our adventures,' said Jack, as he stroked his bow across a block of rosin so it would play smoothly. 'I call it "A Quester's Life". I hope you like it.' He cleared his throat, attacked the strings with the bow and began to sing:

Oh, a quester's life is a jolly life, although it may
be short
We're on the run; it's lots of fun, with a foe in
every port

Even dear old Aunty Millie makes our life quite fraught

And we'll hang on high 'neath the starry sky, if by

pirates we are caught

Ohhhhh, we'll hang on high and must say goodbye,

if by pirates we are caught.

'I'm sorry,' interrupted Trundle. 'Is that supposed to cheer us up? Because if it is, then you've seriously misjudged your audience.'

Jack frowned at him, his bow falling still. 'Everyone's a critic these days,' he sighed.